MY GRANDMOTHER'S EYES

By Carol Gabourie Cooper

PublishAmerica
Baltimore

ISBN: 1-60813-014-2
PUBLISHED BY PUBLISHAMERICA, LLLP
www.publishamerica.com
Baltimore

Printed in the United States of America

I dedicate this book to my grandchildren and youth encouraging them to maintain high ideals, and to love and respect themselves and others.

I thank God for my many blessings and that I have lived long enough to realize a dream.

Thanks to PublishAmerica staff for your guidance. I look forward to a long successful relationship.

Thanks Joseph, my husband, for your forbearance in reading many drafts and for being chief cook and thanks to my family who tried to protect me when they said, "Mom, you are really writing for fun, aren't you?"

"More than fun,' for the love of writing and to fill a desire recognized by writing friends, Claire Mackay and Linda Dionne who critiqued. I thank them and all my friends who had faith in me and spurred me on.

1

My face burned from the sting of the cold wind and my own exhilaration as I clasped Brad around his waist and hung on as though my life depended on him.

I had ignored Dad's well-meant warnings. 'Katie, I know you are too smart a girl to ever get on the back of Brad's motorcycle. That red 'Indian' bike must be over thirty years old. His Dad, Clancy, tore all over the place on that bike. He wiped out on Town Line Road when it was gravel and was all banged up. Lucky for him he wasn't killed.' Mom had agreed but smiled to herself. I suspect she had had a ride or two on the back of Clancy Shaughnessy's bike.

Our ride began a block west of Brad's house in Oshawa. We followed Rossland to Thornton, turned north then east on Conlon the most exciting part of the ride where the road dipped before the bridge over Corbett Creek. Swirling snow blurred our vision. Suddenly we started to slide. Ice on the bridge! Brad wrenched the bike back in control. We tore up the hill, turned at Durham College and headed south on Simcoe Street and back to Rossland Road.

Tingling with excitement, I got off the bike and said. "Now it's my turn!"

"Not on your life, Katie! Your Dad would kill me if I ever let you drive this motorcycle and my Dad would also kill me for letting you."

"Brad," I laughed. "You can't be double-killed."

"Maybe not, but I'd never get to ride Dad's bike again."

"Please, Brad, please. I *will* be careful, I promise. There's no traffic.

You let me ride on the trail off Meadow Crescent. I know how to ride for Pete's sake…just up to the corner and I'll turn around and come right back."

"Okay, since there's no traffic. But it'll soon be dark, so remember, Katie, just to the corner and back."

Brad dismounted and held the bike for me to get on. I leaned over, pecked his cheek and said, "Thanks, Brad. I'll be careful."

I turned at Simcoe as promised and saw Brad less than a block away waiting for me. The wind blew on my face and I screamed a triumphant "Awesome!" My scream stuck somewhere and merged with an explosion and a blinding light. I hovered above the smashed Indian Motorcycle and my own body, crumpled in the snow bank against the shrubbery.

Brad's screams echoed and somehow mingled with the screams and sobs of an old woman. She was leaning over my body, crying. Milk seeped from a broken carton. A loaf of bread lay where she had knelt on it. "No! No!" She cried as people ran from their houses, "Not me darlin', Katie."

"KATIE! KATIE!" Brad screamed, ran to me and knelt down beside my body opposite the old woman. "Call an ambulance!" He shouted. "For God's sake, hurry! Call an ambulance! SOMEBODY, CALL AN AMBULANCE! Dear God, please help her! Help my darling, Katie!"

I floated as in a trance above blaring sirens from arriving ambulance, fire trucks, 'Emergency Measures' truck and police cruisers.

"Over here!" yelled Brad. "Hurry! She's over here!"

The ambulance backed up. Paramedics jumped out with B.P. gauge and a stethoscope. The old woman, who had been crying over me, suddenly gasped, clutched her chest and fell backwards into the snow, her hand stretched toward my body.

"George! Radio for another ambulance." said one paramedic. "An old woman's down beside the explosion victim, looks like a M.I.! Mike, check the woman's pulse. I'll take care of the girl."

The old woman's face was blue against the snow and streaked with eerie flashes of red from the burning house across the street. I recognized her. She was the crossing guard when I was in St. Paul's elementary school.

"Gently now," said Dan checking my blood pressure gauge, "She's very low. I think we might be losing her."

"NO! NO!" Brad screamed. "It can't be! Oh, Dear God, please! It's my fault! I never should've let her ride. Don't die, Katie! DEAR GOD, PLEASE! DON'T LET IT BE SO! "

I was aware of being in an ambulance and heard someone say, "Her B.P. and pulse are dangerously low, George, radio trauma, we're out o' here! Hey, are you her boy friend? If so, start prayin', Bud."

Once again, I floated upwards and hovered above the ambulance, through the emergency entrance and above a stretcher and nothing! I was nowhere that I recognized. I drifted like smoke in a sea of red and hovered, a vaporous nonentity between the warmth of the hospital bed and the chill of the unknown. I felt the presence of someone I should know but whom I had never met…yet a friendly presence who entered my subconscious.

∗∗

"Katie, I have given you the gift of me eyes. "

∗∗

The explosion! The explosion that had thrown me unconscious to the ground; the explosion that had propelled me into another dimension, exiting and hovering over Lake Ridge Hospital. The presence is still with me and I said. "My eyes! After the accident, I was blind. Now I see red. Am I dead?"

∗∗

"No, darlin'. Yer not dead. You'll see again when yer bandages are removed. You'll see through me eyes. I willed them to the eye bank. When I saw you, hurt in the snow, I had a heart attack and died. Little did I know when I willed me eyes that me own granddaughter would get them. "

∗∗

"My Grandmother Regan, Dad's mother. I never knew you! I never knew anything about you, except you went away and didn't come back."

***

"I did go away. Memories were too painful here for me to stay so I went to Ireland. I still had ties there and wanted to go back. There I decided to go by Mrs. Patrick O'Neil, the name I had when I left there many years ago when I was eighteen. The trip was a great disappointment. Our little cottage by the sea was the worse for wear. Brambles grew against the windowpanes and the door hung open on rusted hinges. Friends I had left behind had either died or moved on. I returned to Canada. It was too painful to live in me little house on Meadow Road in Whitby, the house where Greg's anger still reverberated in me ears. I locked the doors, paid the taxes and rented an apartment in a seniors' building."

***

"I…I don't understand. Why would dad be so angry with his own mother? What happened to cause such a rift that I never got to know you?"

***

"Yer da, Greg, is me first-born and only child by yer grand da, Sean Gregory Regan. Eric's mither, Mary Ellen Farrell, died givin' birth to him and Sean raised him with the help of Mrs. Flood. She and her husband rented rooms above Regan's Hardware Store. She minded Eric from birth until he was six years old.

When the Floods moved to Orillia, I took over and cared for Eric and worked beside yer grand da, Sean. Yer uncle, Eric, was raised in that store, the darlin' of all the customers and the apple of Sean's eye. I married Sean Regan. A year later yer da, Greg, was born when Eric was eight."

***

"Grandmother, I still don't understand why Dad never came back. If he was your son, why didn't you try harder to make it right between you? What happened to cause such a rift?"

***

"Me darlin', Katie, yer grand da loved your da very much but he favored Eric. Business prospered and Sean planned to leave all three stores to Eric. I tried to convince

him to leave at least one store to Greg but he was adamant. He banged the table and yelled, 'I've made up me mind, Emma, and me will, and that's the end of it. Don't ever mention it again! I've left the house to you. Me investments are more than ample to see Greg through university, if he wishes.' He patted me hand and said, 'You'll see, Emma, that I've been fair.'

I knew he'd never change his mind so to keep peace I let it be."

***

"But, Grandmother, it's not like Dad to hold a grudge nor was it the way I was raised. He never talked about you or his childhood. I never even saw your picture."

***

"Greg was distraught by his da's death, as was I, but he was devastated when all stores were left to Eric, even though funds were secured for him to deal with life as he saw fit but he cut me off.

'I'm his son too,' he had shouted. 'I'm your only son, by birth! You should've got Dad to change the will. It's your fault! Eric will never keep the business! He wants to be a doctor! That still leaves me with beggar all! Did Dad think I'd become a janitor and sweep Eric's floors like I did for him as a kid?'

I tried to get Greg to be reasonable and to see that funds had been provided for his college, but his anger overrode his reason. I was cut to the quick when he yelled, 'Some mother you are to place your stepson before your own flesh and blood!'

***

"But, that was such a long time ago."

***

"Be patient, darlin' girl. Yer a little like yer da, the impatient part. I told Greg. 'I know yer angry and you know in yer heart that it won't come to that. You wont want, Greg. I'll see to that. He's provided for you.' 'Yeah, he said, 'Just like you didn't see to Dad's will. I don't want or need his damned charity. I'll make it on my own without any help from him or you. You'll see!'

Greg ignored me tears and shook me hand from his arm. He slammed the door and walked out of me life foriver. Yer parents weddin' picture was in the paper and later yer birth announcement, Katie Rita Regan. I knew you were premature so I volunteered to be a rockin' granny just to get a chance to see you in the incubator. I

11

marveled at your perfection. One day Nurse Alma asked, 'Would you like to rock this preemie, Mrs. Regan?' Ah, Katie, the feelin' of ecstasy when I hugged yer newness to me. I snuggled me nose into yer downy hair and breathed in yer sweet baby smells. Me heart beat with love and gratitude for the privilege of holdin' and rockin' you. I thanked God and prayed that yer Guardian Angel would watch over me darlin', Katie. Me euphoria was short-lived. The next day, I scanned every crib and the nurse said, "Oh, baby Katie, she was a real sweetie. She went home this morning…hospital policy, you know.' I was crestfallen. I had held you only once and had worried about your size. 'I know, dear,' said the nurse pattin' me arm. 'Little Katie is stronger than you think. She'll be fine."

***

"I don't feel *fine* right now, floating up here with you in some sort of limbo. I really don't know how I'm here or if I'll ever go back home. I'm mystified by your appearance."

***

'Me darlin', Katie, life is a mystery and so is this in between. You will understand. After me letdown, when you went home early, I vowed I'd be as close to you as I could. That's when I became a crossin' guard at St. Paul's School."

***

"I remember. Brad had a crush on me even then. He's still a tease. He had pushed his way through the other students to stand beside me. It's strange but I feel Brad's nearness."

***

"That's so, Katie, he's yer kindred spirit." She chuckled. "He had jostled you off of the curb and I snatched you back before that on-comin' car."

***

"Brad seems so far away."

***

"He's closer than you think. Try to relax, Katie, while I go on with me story. Do you remember yer soccer games?"

***

"Yes, I was forward on 'The Green Gaels' team. You always cheered for me."

12

***

"That I did, and Mrs. Riley wasn't very pleased. 'Emma,' she'd say, 'me own granddaughter, Moira, is on the yellow team and yer cheerin' for that girl on the Green Gaels Team.' I'd just laugh and say, 'Oh Mary, I cheers for them all.'"

Mavournin, and a sweeter colleen there niver was at yer graduation, like a wee 'faerie' princess,' that you were in yer pale green dress and yer long dark tresses piled on yer head. It gave me heart a blessin' just to be there."

***

I laughed at the way she expressed herself and said, "Grandma, I'm sorry I never had you to love and tell me stories."

***

"You have, me now, darlin', but to get on with me story, I wasn't invited to yer graduation, of course, but I volunteered to help with the lunch. I wore glasses and had dyed me hair red and kept in the background. I'd never met yer mither. When yer da had his back turned talkin' with the principal I passed you a serviette after you spilled yer punch. I was afraid that Greg might recognize me. I didn't want to spoil yer evenin' so I watched from the doorway when he took you in his arms."

***

"You were there! I remember someone had bumped into Brad and I had laughed and said, 'Not his fault.' Then I danced with Dad."

***

"Yes, Katie, I watched you and after a few moments I slipped out through the kitchen and didn't see you again 'til the accident."

***

"The accident! My eyes, 'MY GRANDMOTHER'S EYES'!" I said in renewed wonder. What a waste of the good times we might have had. Poor, Grandma, all the hurts and all those years and I never even got to meet you."

***

"Yer meetin' me now, Mavournin. We've a bond. We'll meet again very soon."

***

"Soon. soon," I murmured . Her presence floated away from me and I drifted down to the warmth of my hospital bed. "Oh, Grandma, Grandma!…I'm so sorry…so sorry."

A man's voice invaded my subconscious. "She's coming round. She's trying to speak. Katie! Katie! Can you hear me? Wake up, Katie!"

Warm hands massaged my hands and feet. I fluttered to awareness and an envelope of white surrounded me.

"We're here, dear," said Mom.

"Thank, God!" Dad said.

"Gently, gently nurse," said the male voice.

I struggled to regain consciousness suspended between the presence that I had just left and this new yet familiar place. "Sorry…sorry…my eyes, your eyes?" I was aware of a blinding light and my lips moving but I couldn't speak.

"Relax, Katie." The male voice was Dr. MacLean. "I just want to get a look at your beautiful peepers."

My eyes felt moist. Someone blotted the excess liquid from my cheeks. Again, the blinding white light made me wince.

"Very good," said Dr. MacLean, scanning the light in both eyes. "In fact, excellent. God, bless your eye bank donor whoever he or she may be."

My mouth quivered into a smile and once again, I was aware of Grandmother Regan, closer than ever. I seemed to float in and out of consciousness, aware of something, above and beyond and then the more familiar awareness of caressing hands and loving voices

2

It has been a month since my accident and what everyone is calling a miraculous recovery. My eyes appear to be more of a hazel-green now. 'Just like Mom's,' said Dad. That was the first time I had ever heard him refer to his mother.

Confusing thoughts tortured me. I pushed the surreal presence of Grandmother Regan O'Neil into the recesses of my mind. The purpose of life and how I fit into it puzzles me. Who am I? What is my destiny?

Sometimes I have flashbacks to early childhood and the relative freedom of country life, the pets I had and the mystery of life watching farm animals. Mom took me into the house when a stallion was trotted down our lane to the whinnying mare behind the barn. When our cat had kittens on my bed, I pressed to know how they got inside of Muffy since she didn't have a husband.

Mysteries of life unfolded. As I went through grade school, I had minor crushes but for the most part having girl friends and taking part in school life was my main concern. I was happy and was encouraged to take pride in myself and to be grateful for the gifts God gave me. Family, friends and loyalties shared gave me a sense of security. My marks were average, except for math. My confidence was boosted when I excelled in volleyball and swimming. I flipped the pages of my diary until I came to 'HIGH SCHOOL ORIENTATION.'

High school did little to prepare me for the first day in grade nine, a shocker to be alone in a sea of students. I finally found my homeroom. No one in my class was from St. Paul's School. Mr. Farquarson held a clipboard, called attendance and assigned locker numbers. I scanned each face, casting for a hoped-for friend. Nancy Freeman's hand went up for locker seventy-six.

Matt Dennis stood for locker seventy-seven and said. "Yo! I'm your man!"

That broke the tension and the class laughed.

"A simple *present* will do, Dennis."

Matt bowed several times and we laughed louder.

"Perhaps you should join 'Theatre Arts' where you can give full expression to your talents, Dennis," said Mr. Farquarson.

Matt looked at me and winked. I blushed and looked at my desk. Finally, my name was called for locker seventy-eight. Nancy turned around and smiled. We crowded through the door and I found my locker. I fumbled with the lock, dropped it and my books and bent to pick them up. A bump from behind caused me to hit my head on the locker. I stared at the scruffy joggers and up jean-glad legs to the grinning face of the class clown.

"Sorry! Are you hurt?"

"Huh? No, I'm fine."

"Matt, Matt Dennis." He lifted me up by my elbows until we were eyelevel and grinned.

"Yes, yes I know. Would you please set me down? Everyone's staring!"

"Way to go, Matt! Sweepin' her off her feet before she gets a chance to run the other way," said a girl in high black boots and a leather mini. She gave Matt the hip and he spun around shielding me from a second blow to the locker and set me back on my feet. She walked away wiggling her tush, a long chain swinging from her belt.

"Give it a rest, Frieda! What're you tryin' to do, give the school a bad name, struttin' your stuff like a Halloween witch?"

Frieda turned back and made rude tongue-wiggles at Matt. She stuck her nose in the air and strutted down the hall. Nancy had her mouth open and I was shaking, not so much by Frieda, but at Matt's closeness. My mouth was dry and I needed to find the fountain. Matt picked up my books and linked arms with Nancy and me.

"Forget about freaky Frieda! She used to date my bro, but I guess he was too tame for her. Now, she's pissed and takes it out on anyone he or I am with. I'll show you gals 'round."

And, so he did. Matt was popular, very often the centre in a crowd of jostling admirers. Matt made me laugh. He was a good dancer and kisser too, my first real boyfriend and my best friend all through grades nine and ten. I cheered for him in track and field. Most of our dates were with Nancy and one of Matt's friends or with groups to sports events, teen dances or beach parties. He was getting hard to resist with his teasing, laughing ways, especially when his kisses went from my mouth, to my neck, to my breasts. I had plans for my life and even though he thrilled me to bits. I joked off his advances and struggled with my own hormones until that swimming party at the lake.

It was Labor Day weekend and we had squeezed out the last hours of summer. A group of us had spent all day on a secluded beach. Our gang had gone but Matt had built a campfire and we stayed for just one more swim. Matt chased me into the waves and caught me. He picked me up and ran laughing back to our blanket. The sun had set. I clung to him, kissed his neck and said, "Matt, I'm freezing!"

"Katie, my girl, old Matt will warm you up."

He lay on top of me and pulled the blanket up around us. I clung to his warmth, basked in his kisses and love. He got playful and blew on my cheeks making blubbering noises that sent shivers all the way through me. The more I laughed the sillier he got until I said, "Stop! Stop! You're tickling me to death! I'm warm enough!"

Suddenly he stopped. His eyes glowed in the firelight. His heat throbbed through me. I churned with arousal when I felt him grow hard against me.

He looked me in the eyes and said. "Please, Katie, you know I love you." He fumbled in his knapsack.

"I know, Matt, *but no!* It's not what I want…not what I planned, not what we planned…not like this!"

"You know you want me as much as I want you…just this once! Please! We'll be bound together! Look! I brought a condom. It'll be okay, I promise!"

"Matt, NO! Please, Matt, I love you too but I'm not ready. I've plans for my future. You do too! We can't spoil it by rushing…"

"*Rushing! Rushing!* Katie, we've been going steady for a year, and I've wanted you from the first time I saw you. I know you want me too."

He rolled off me, and sat up. I put my arm around him and said, "Oh, Matt, I do want you! Life is so unfair! All these wonderful feelings but I'm not ready. It's just too soon for me to have you or anyone else. Please understand, Matt. I have to finish school, maybe college and then I want to marry and have my own family. I don't want to ruin my life like poor Frieda. She's only fifteen and she's already had an abortion and bragging about how there's nothing to it. I can't go down that road. *I won't!*" I started to cry and Matt rocked me like a baby.

"It's not like that, Katie. Not with us, and *you are not* like Frieda or anyone like her. I love you for who you are, Katie, and for the love you've given me. Hey! You're my best girl! You're right! Life seems unfair but we'll work things out for the best. Now," and he gave me a kiss on my cheek, "I'd better get you home before your dad unleashes his Irish temper on me."

"And before I get grounded for a year," I said.

Steaks were on the menu for an end-of-summer Bar B. Q. but we were two hours late and my parents had waited for us. When Matt begged off with the excuse being 'last-minute things to get ready for school,' Dad raised his eyebrow but said nothing. Usually, Matt wasn't shy about scooping me up in front of my parents and planting a loud lip-smacker and afterwards he would set me down, laugh and say, 'Just like liftin' a sack o' spuds.' But that night he wrapped me in his arms and gave me a chaste kiss on the top of my head.

We still dated off and on but not on our own. I ached for him. It hurt so much when he dated other girls that I changed schools for grade eleven. At Paul Dwyer, I dove into school activities, still aching for Matt and finding no answers to 'What ifs? I enjoyed a few plutonic double dates with my friend, Siobhan, and her present crush.

***

A knock on my bedroom door coincided with my need to blow my nose.

"Katie, are you all right?"

I realized that if had been crying but answered, "I…I'm fine. Mom." I set my diary down and dabbed my teardrops on the page.

She opened my door a crack. "I heard you crying. Katie. Dear, are you in pain?"

"No…Yes…I'm so confused. I hardly know what I want or even who I am anymore."

"Ah, my poor girl." Her empathy opened the floodgates and I rushed sobbing into her arms. "There, there, Katie. Come and sit down. I've made ginger tea." Ginger tea, the Regan fixer-upper brought a smile through my tears. "There now," said Mom, "that's better." We sipped our tea and I looked over the brim of my cup at my dear mother. She was always there for me.

"More tea, Katie?"

My cup refilled, I said, "Mom, I've been reading about events in my life and questioning who I am and why am I here? Re-hashing my life in my diary shouldn't be so traumatic, years after the events, but since my accident and my out-of-body experience, I want to grab life *now!* I don't want to mess up but I don't want to wait for Brad until he's graduated from Queen's, either."

Mom smiled. "I know exactly how you feel."

"You do?"

"Yes, dear, *I really do!* I'm sure many couples struggle with that decision."

"Even you and Dad?"

"Yes, Katie, even us."

"But…but…I don't understand. You always taught me to take pride in myself, to wait for marriage and yet…yet?

"I know, dear, but as parents we wanted you to have more for yourself than we had before we took that step."

"But you and Dad are happy, aren't you?"

"Very happy, even blissfully so. We were so in love, but our being in love and getting pregnant out of wedlock was very scandalous in the fifties. Even insurance companies withheld coverage if the couple had not been married for ten months. You see Katie, worse than financial difficulties, there was the emotional strain. I was living at home and Papa threatened to throw me out of the house. 'You've brought disgrace to the family name to say nothin' on Mother Church.' Nona tried to intervene but Papa was old country. 'There was enough of that in those war years,' he said. 'We came here for a new start, with nothin'. *No! No, Gina, I wont have it!* We wanted better for you!'

Greg worked at a lumber company. We took two rooms and I cleaned house for the landlady.

Somehow we managed but it wasn't easy without our parents backing. Greg never spoke of his parents except to say, 'They're gone, Gina, and I can't talk about it.' We were happy, and so busy trying to make ends meet that my only concern was for the life I carried, you, Katie. After you were born, Papa had-a-change-of-heart, and I was welcomed back into the family.

If you and Brad really love each other, Katie, we trust you to follow *your hearts* and make the decision that is right for you. We can't tell you how to live your life. We hope better for you than what we had. We want what is *best for you*, whatever you decide."

20

3

A registered letter addressed to Mr. Gregory Sean Regan and Miss Katie Rita Regan came from the office of H.G. Dunbar, Barrister and Solicitor, requesting us to see him as soon as I was well enough. Dad, as manager of House and Home Lumber, managed to get off work early for the mystery appointment.

Two o'clock, Thursday, Mr. Dunbar greeted us warmly and with sympathy, "So sorry to hear of your mother's death, Mr. Regan...and at the same time as your daughter's accident."

Color drained from Dad's face. I thought he was going to faint.

"Here, here, sit down, Mr. Regan!" He turned to his secretary and said, "Rose, please hurry and bring Mr. Regan a glass of water. Better still bring the thermos and two glasses."

"My...my mother? I didn't know. We...we...I...lost touch...I...I..."

I felt so sorry for Dad. My heart was breaking for him.

Mr. Dunbar's face turned pink. "I'm so sorry, Mr. Regan. I didn't...I thought you knew."

Dad recovered somewhat and said, "My...our daughter." He took my hand. "We were so concerned for Katie."

"Yes, yes," said Mr. Dunbar. "I understand."

Dad continued as though in a trance. He seemed to be trying to digest what Mr. Dunbar had said and at the same time he looked embarrassed not knowing of the death of his own mother and said,

"You see, Mr. Dunbar, Gina and I practically lived at the hospital. We took turns sleeping on a cot in Katie's room. I..."

I patted Dad's shaking hand and said, "Perhaps, Dad, another day would be better." Since my encounter with my grandmother's presence, I feared that the will might cause him further trauma.

"I'm fine, Katie." Dad squeezed my hand and said, "Mr. Dunbar, please proceed."

"Very well. I represented your mother's legal affairs and today I want to read her last will to her sole beneficiaries, you, Greg and Katie."

I glanced at Dad. He cleared his throat and gulped more water while Mr. Dunbar read:

I, Emma Louise Regan (O'Neil) bequeath to my first-born and only son, Gregory Seam Regan the original Regan's Hardware store, 368 Simcoe St. South, Oshawa, Ontario, and all the contents of said property. I further bequeath the sum of one hundred thousand dollars to update and re-stock said property.

Dad shook. He grabbed the glass and drained its contents. Mr. Dunbar signaled his secretary for refills and said, "Do you want me to continue, Mr. Regan?"

Dad cleared his throat. "Yes, please...please continue."

I, Emma Louise Regan O'Neil bequeath to my only granddaughter, Katie Rita Regan my little house and contents on 51 Meadow Road, Whitby, Ontario, my jewelry and my car, a Pontiac Grand Am purchased 1989. I also bequeath the sum of eighty thousand dollars to be invested and withdrawn as needed to assist Katie's education either in university or the college of her choice. I bequeath an additional five thousand dollars for care and maintenance of the aforementioned property.

All legal and probate fees will be deducted from my estate. Mr. Dunbar and Rose Forestall have signed and witnessed this, my Last Will and Testament.

"Mrs. Regan left these personal letters for you, Greg and Katie," said Mr. Dunbar.

Tears rolled down our faces and dotted the papers necessary for the release of the will. Somehow, we made the short distance home in shocked silence. I felt the presence of Grandmother Emma Regan O'Neil.

We entered the house and barely acknowledged Mom waiting to serve dinner. Dad went to his corner office and sat with his head in his hands while I went to my room anxious to read her letter. I opened it with trembling fingers and read with blurring vision the same words her presence had revealed. Words jumped from the page....*soccer...graduation,* more than déjà vu. A rap on my door seemed far off, a distant echo.

"Katie, Katie, please open the door. May I come in?"

"Oh, Dad. I don't know how to explain, it's just..."

"You don't have to explain anything, Katie." Dad sat on my bed and passed me a tissue. I clutched my grandmother's letter, afraid that if I put it down that she would go away again and said, "Everything's a mystery."

"I know, dear, a sad mystery but, Katie, darling, there's nothing we can do about the past. Don't mourn so. You never even knew your grandmother."

"And *whose* fault is that? It's *your* fault! IT'S ALL YOUR FAULT! That's whose fault it is! YOURS! YOURS ALONE! You always put me off when I asked about her and you *never even showed me her picture. You, Dad, robbed me of knowing and having a loving grandmother....your very own mother. HOW COULD YOU?*" Dad put his arm over my shoulder but I brushed it away and continued to strike out. "*I DON'T* CARE WHAT YOU THOUGHT! You don't know the half of it!" I hiccupped..."Not even a little bit! LEAVE ME ALONE!"

"Darling, girl! My darling, Katie, I know more than you think. Rest for now. Dinner can wait. We'll talk more about it later. I want to share my letter with you and your mother."

I lay back, clutching my letter. Dad draped the afghan over me and quietly left my room. A feeling of peace and a sense of my grandmother's presence pervaded my being.

***

"Don't grieve so. I still watch over you and Greg. He needs yer understandin'. Rest now, Katie and say the Lord's Prayer. You'll feel better."

***

Grandmother's words ebbed into and comforted me. I must have slept as I awoke somewhat refreshed. I washed my face, went to the kitchen and gave Mom a hug. She looked at me, a question in her eyes, but said nothing and gave Dad a worried glance. He smiled a tentative welcome at me as though he didn't know how I'd react after my outburst.

"Dinner's ready whenever you are. Greg. I've made your favorite, lasagna."

Dad barely acknowledged Mom. I went to him and kissed the top of his head. "C'mon, Dad. Mom's been waiting hours. She's really worried."

"Oh, yes of course. Coming, Gina," he said, "Dinner smells wonderful, as usual."

We made the sign of the cross and held hands. It was Dad's turn to say the blessing. "Thank you, Lord, for the safe return of our dear daughter, Katie." He glanced at me smiled and continued. "And please give me the grace of forgiveness as we know you forgive us. Bless this food and our family."

"And thank you, God, for Grandmother Regan O'Neil."

Mom raised her eyebrows and looked at me as though I had had a relapse but said nothing and started to cut the lasagna.

I broke the silence. "M-m-m good, Mom." Something strange is going on with Dad. He usually says, Thanks, God, for this food and all here present. Gina, please pass the potatoes,' or whatever.

"How was your meeting with Mr. Dunbar? Is everything okay at work, Greg?"

"Uh, fine, Gina. Everything's fine at work."

"What is it, Greg? Both you and Katie have been so upset since your meeting. Maybe I can help if you tell me what's bothering you."

"Nothing's wrong, Gina." Dad snapped uncharacteristically and Mom's eyes welled with tears. "I'm sorry, Gina." Dad reached over and squeezed her hand. Mom slowly lowered the lasagna to Dad's plate.

Lilting Irish songs had been playing in the background. When the melancholy strains of Danny Boy,' Dad's favorite, began to play, Dad abruptly got up and said, "Do you mind if I change that one, Gina? We need to hear something more cheerful."

I picked at my food and Mom asked, "Katie, dear, are you sure you're feeling all right, the lasagna too spicy? I'll heat stew if you like."

Overwhelmed by the events of the day, Mom's kind sympathy set me into another spate of sorrow. I blurted, "May I please be excused?" I bolted for the bathroom, closed the door and shook with renewed sobs.

This time, Mom knocked on the door. "Come on out, sweetie, and we'll talk when you're ready. I fixed you a cup of green tea with ginger, just the way you like it."

I opened the door, and fell into Mom's arms and cried, "Oh, Mom, now she's gone and I never knew her. I never even got to see her. I don't even have a picture of her."

"Who's gone, dear? Did one of your friends die?

"Don't you know? Didn't Dad tell you?"

"Tell me what's the matter, dear. I don't understand."

"Oh no, Mom, you don't know! That's why you asked all those questions at the table. Grandmother is dead and I didn't get to see her."

"Sweetheart, your grandmother died three years ago."

"I don't mean Nona Veltri. I mean Grandmother Regan O'Neil."

"But dear, you must have had a bad dream. You don't have a Grandmother O'Neil and you never met your Dad's mother. Everything has just been too much for you, the accident, the lawyer," said Mom, a frown creasing her forehead.

"Yes, I do! I really do have a Grandmother O'Neil! She was Dad's

25

Mom! She changed her name back to O'Neil after the argument between her and Dad."

"Honey, you must be confused. The surgery,...you've been through so much."

"We've all been through too much, Gina, much too much," said Dad wrapping his arms around us. "Come, sit down. I've a lot of explaining to do and much forgiving from my poor dear mother. May God forgive me for preventing you from knowing her love, Katie" He stifled a sob. "After tea I'll explain what happened at the lawyer's office."

I sipped slowly and let the aroma drift around me. Again, I became aware of my Grandmother Emma Regan O'Neil and a feeling of wellbeing and peace swept over me. I smiled across my cup into my parents' eyes and knew that our filial love would prevail.

Dad was the first to speak and said as he gave the letter to Mom. "Before I tell you about the will, Gina, I want to share this letter from my mother, the mother I prevented you both, God forgive me," he stifled a sob..."from meeting let alone knowing. It will help us all to understand. Go ahead, Gina, read the letter."

***

Eric sold the two newer Regan's Hardware stores, enabling him to complete his medical studies and to set up practice in Boston. Eric, dismayed by the breakup of our family signed the first Regan's Hardware over to me to keep for you, Greg, when you were ready to accept the offer.

I set my cup on the table and watched Mom as she read the letter and occasionally whispered Grandmother Regan O'Neil's words.

"Oh, Greg! How terrible! If only we had known, then perhaps Katie and I could have eased the way for you to reconcile with your mother."

"Our parting was so painful," said Dad. "At first I was so hurt and angry that my father had left all three stores to Eric that I stubbornly blamed Mom. Time went on and I felt she didn't even miss me because she had Eric."

"Where's Eric now? Did he come to your mother's funeral?" "I must write to Eric in Boston. No, Gina. Mom didn't want a funeral. She chose cremation. She didn't deserve the hurt I gave her, *especially* in not giving her the chance to know and love Katie, her only granddaughter."

"Don't worry, Dad. She forgives you and everyone. I have her eyes."

"Yes dear, there's a resemblance in personality but you have your own eyes."

"Not since the accident. Grandmother Regan O'Neil told me when I was in the hospital, that I have her eyes. I have Grandmother Regan O'Neil's eyes."

"Darling, Katie. you've been through too much and probably had a dream. You said all sorts of strange things for a time after you came out of your coma. Remember our visit with Mr Dunbar. He gave us a copy of her death certificate. She died while you were in hospital."

"If you say so, Dad. Would you like me to read her letter?"

Mom interrupted my reading. "When we took you home from the nursery, the nurse on duty commented that babies who are rocked and cuddled have a better chance of survival. To think that your grandmother was your rocking granny." Mom sniffed and poured more tea. "And, soccer; I remember the crossing guard lady cheering for you. I saw her at your graduation. I would've welcomed her with open arms."

Dad muffled a sob and went into the bathroom. Mom sat in stunned silence until Dad came back in the room and said, "Ah, Gina! I knew you would have. I was just so darned stubborn. Mom used to say, 'Greg, yer so stubborn you'd cut off yer nose to spite yer face.' She was right. I'll make it up to you in every way I can, Katie. I promise."

"There, there, Greg dear," said Mom.

I felt a soft nudge from her presence and said, "I know you will, Dad. I know you will."

We sat for a bit, just being family and Dad passed the will to Mom who said after reading, "Oh, Greg and Katie, such forgiveness! I feel enveloped by love. The letters, this room has an aura of heavenly

27

freshness as though your Mom was with us. If only I'd known I would have loved her as my own mother."

"I know, Gina," said Dad, visibly shaken by the letters and the will. "It'll take me a lifetime to forgive myself for being so stubborn and loosing the treasure I had in my mother's love and the supreme sacrifice I caused her in not having Katie be a part of her life"

"I know she forgives you, Dad, so you'll have to forgive yourself."

"Easier said than done and to think she kept the store for me all these years. I find it over-whelming to comprehend her loss, her death and the will. We will need much time to adjust to these changes, and of course, I'll have to give Mr. Jensen ample notice at work."

"I'm sure your assistant is very capable, Greg."

"That he is, Gina. And now, Katie, what else do you have in that bulky envelope?"

I ran to my room and dumped snapshots and a photo album, over my bed and whooped. Mom and Dad rushed to help me gather everything, and with shaking hands we took them to the table.

Grandfather Sean Gregory Regan and his first wife, Mary Ellen smiled from their wedding picture of May 23, 1942.

The picture of baby Eric in the arms of his dad moved us to tears when Dad said, "Mary Ellen had died giving birth to him. This next picture is Mrs. Flood with Eric.

"Grandma told me about Mrs. Flood," I said then asked, "Is that you, Dad? It looks like Granddad's holding a ham."

"He's holding a ham all right." Mom nudged Dad, "And, he's still a ham."

"Hey! Who do you think you're calling a ham?"

"You," said Mom. "The same guy who pours a stream of coffee as long as his arm into the coffee pot."

"Perambulator? Looks like a cage."

"Oh, I get it, Katie, you're ganging up on me, eh? One time, I slipped out of my harness, and climbed over the end of that buggy and slid down until my toes touched the floor. I grabbed a bag of licorice and hid behind the counter. Mom saw my shoe sticking out and me covered in black from head to foot. After that my harness was buckled at the back."

"Now who's the 'Corker,' Dad?"

"I was and a very sick one. After that episode, candy was displayed on an upper shelf. This is my 'First Holy Communion' picture. I balked at those short pants and this is Eric at his 'Confirmation.' Here's Eric arm over my shoulder, bat and ball ready for a game of pick-up."

"He looks pretty cool with his baseball cap on sideways," I said.

"Eric was about fourteen. I idolized him and followed him every chance I got. We played catch and pick-up. He used to ruffle my hair and say, 'Someday, Sport, you're going t' be a great ball player.' When I went to grade school, Eric had moved on but his good student reputation hounded me all the way through school. I was restless, always cracking jokes, the class clown."

"And we know why, don't we, Mom?"

"Go ahead you too, laugh. Our coach encouraged me and said I could go pro if I worked at it."

"So, Dad, what happened with the baseball idea?"

"When I reached high school I had a profound interest in the opposite sex, particularly for the ravishing, Gina Veltri." He looked at Mom who blushed. "I lacked the effort to make big time."

"Oh, Greg! I'm the one who made it big when I married you and had Katie."

Dad smiled and said, "Being happy didn't put food on the table. I got a regular job at a lumber company and worked part time at a grocery store. The doors were locked forever, and my hoped-for plans for Regan's Hardware were dashed when I thought Eric had sold the business. He had gone to study medicine in Boston with plans on becoming a gynecologist. He had said, 'I want to save women from what happened to Mom.' I never dreamed that one day the original Regan's Hardware would be willed back to me and that has changed everything, right, ladies?"

"Right!" Mom and I said in unison and she continued, "You know, Greg, I'm looking forward to working alongside of you. I think your father did you the bigger favor, more than you then realized. You were too young to take on the responsibility of running the hardware. Now as an experienced manager at House and Home Lumber. Regan's Hardware should be a snap. When are we to begin your new venture?"

"*Our* new venture, Gina. First, I need to tell Mr. Jensen. Construction is booming so he'll need to supervise our spring shipment."

"Imagine, Dad, returning to the same Regan's Hardware where you swept floors as a youth."

"Yes, and I also remember sorting bins of nuts, bolts and stocking shelves."

"Greg, if I'd known you missed sweeping floors so much, I would've put you to work."

"Since there's so much work, why don't we go there now?"

"It's getting dark, Katie," said Mom, "and it's been a long and tiring day. Your Dad has the weekend off. So why not wait until Saturday. I think you need a little rest. Perhaps you'd like to invite Siobhan and Tina over for a short visit Friday night."

"Sure, Mom, I'll phone later. I'm pooped!"

"I could sleep for a week," said Dad."

"Me too," said Mom. "Then *it* is settled."

4

Strains of Brahms' Lullaby drifted to me. Dear Mom always played that piece to help me sleep. I smiled at the memory and turned on my reading lamp but couldn't concentrate. Emotions and memories of the day's events blurred the words and my eyes filled with tears.

***

My Grandmother's presence manifested itself. I drifted off and entered another time and place where the surroundings, though new to me, were familiar.

I looked down from the cliff and out to a raging sea and a wind that swirled me hair about me head and billowed me long skirt. I was torn by indecision. Should I remain and get drenched, or should I return to the cottage and await his return? More than common sense but a strange urgency drew me to the cottage.

Back in the cottage, I put more peat in the hearth and stirred the stew in the pot suspended on the hog over the peat fire. The low-beamed ceiling radiated heat back into the room. I lit candles, took biscuits from a crock and wondered how I knew where everything was. I served a bowl of stew for meself and upon taking it to the table. I jolted and spilled hot stew on me hand when I heard,

"Yer me, Emma Louise O'Neil. This cottage belonged to Patrick and me when we were first married."

***

"Oh! Oh!" I cried and awoke with a start. I pulled my hand away from the night-light and staggered into the kitchen for ice. I yanked open the freezer, shook cubes into a tea towel and wrapped my hand. The moon stretched a path across the black and white linoleum floor and over the kitchen table where my grandmother's presence illuminated before me. "Who? Why? I don't understand," I whispered.

***

"Go back to bed, Katie. Go back to bed, darlin'. Yer burn will be healed by mornin'. I had to wake you up before…" Her voice trailed off.

***

"Before what?"

***

"Niver mind now." She smiled. "Patience, me dear. You'll see all in good time."

***

"The dream? Ireland? I was you in Ireland?" My questions were unanswered.

***

"You've been through so much…the accident…my will. You'll see come mornin', darlin' girl."

***

She was gone! That's strange. '*You'll see all in good time' and 'come mornin'.*

***

"Sleep well? I noticed the towel on the kitchen table. Did you get up for a snack?"

My hand was healed. "Huh? No, Mom…probably a leprechaun."

"Oh, Katie, you and your Irish superstitions."

"And *you*, with your silly little ditties." I sang, 'I know a funny little man as quiet as a mouse, who does the mischief that is done in everybody's house.' Must've been *your* funny little man."

"Aw, Katie."

"She's a Corker," said Dad pouring himself a cup of coffee. Then he sang. 'My gal's a Corker…She's a…

Mom and I both cut him off when I said, "Dad, don't you dare compare me to that gal in the song, inferring that I have big feet. *Big feet indeed!*" And, Mom said, "Good glory, Katie!" as she hurried to check the safety locks. She was off on another worrying tangent. "I hope you weren't sleep-walking. You haven't done that since childhood."

"Stop fussing, Gina. We would've heard her," said Dad as he took a last swig of coffee, kissed me on the forehead and Mom on the lips. "Well, I'm off."

"Dad, I thought you were going to take Friday off."

"I was but I want to get everything shipshape before I leave. I'll be off tonight."

I worried. "I hope I can catch up on my homework after missing so much."

"You're a bright gal and will soon catch up with a little tutoring. Brad's home, why not ask him? He was at the hospital every day after your accident repeatedly blaming himself, even though it wasn't completely his fault."

"Poor, Brad, I'll call him."

5

Brad didn't get a chance to ring the doorbell as I'd been watching for him and threw myself into his arms almost knocking him off the porch.

"Whoa! Take it easy!"

"Oh. Brad, I'm sorry! I've missed you so much."

"Aw, my darling Katie. I'm the one who's sorry. I can't believe that I was so stupid. I never should have let you…"

His voice trailed off muffled by my lips and the embrace that almost crushed the daffodils. "Brad, they're beautiful! Thanks so much."

"Katie, *me* love," he wrapped me in his arms. "They'll never match *yer* beauty."

"Hey, you two," yelled Mom. "Come in and close the door. The draft comes all the way to the kitchen. Daffodils, how lovely, Brad. I'll put them in a vase. I know Katie is *dying* to start."

"Umm, thanks, Mom. We can study in my room, Brad. I'm almost ashamed to say that I've barely scanned science and that's where I need your help."

"Any other pressing subjects for this semester, Katie?"

"Not really, I can review English and history on my own. Science is my biggest bug. For this semester I only need to catch up on three main subjects."

"Science it is, then. Oh, ho! What's this? You're diary, Katie?"

"No you don't, Brad Shaughnessy! *That's private!*" I stood on tiptoe trying to take it from him.

"Private, eh? Oh, I get it, it's all about Matt and the crush you had on him. I heard all about it."

"Brad, stop teasing."

"You're blushin', Katie, *me gir-r-l.*"

"Brad, don't try your Irish charm on me. It won't work!"

"Always worked before, though, didn't it?"

"Brad, come on! Give it to me! "He laughed falling back on my bed, pulling me on top of him saying, "I'll give it to you all right, Katie Regan."

He tickled me until I tingled all over and yelled, "Stop, Brad Shaughnessy! Stop this minute! You're incorrigible!" My diary fell to the floor. We clung to each other denying our passion.

Mom called from the kitchen. "Science wasn't that much fun when I went to school."

We laughed like two kids until Brad said, "We're studying domestic science, Mrs. R. Katie has so much to learn that I might have to stay all night."

"In your dreams, Brad Schaughnessy."

"No harm in dreamin', is there, Mrs. R.?"

"No harm at all, *me foin lad.* I didn't think science was one of the romance languages."

"It's all what you make of it, Mrs. R."

I gave Brad a little thump on his chest and made a funny face. I raised my voice. "IF, *you too are finished* with your Irish banter *I* might get some help with science."

"Katie, you little minx! You started the whole thing. Say, am I in that diary, or not?"

"Of course you are. I might let you read it...sometime."

"Might? Sometime?"

"Yes, Brad. I don't have any secrets from you. You're not the only one who likes to tease, but *today,"* I said briskly, putting my diary in the drawer, *"we're studying science."*

"Okay, okay!" Brad raised his hands in defeat. "We'd better straighten your bed." We faced each other across my bed. Brad snapped the covers over our heads, brought them down over us like a tent and said, "Let's play doctor." We fell back on the bed laughing. Brad grabbed me by the shoulders. "Open your mouth, Katie. I'm your dentist."

My laugh muffled in the covers until we untangled ourselves and finally straightened the bedding. "Brad, you're a Corker."

"No, Katie, you are."

"Let's face it," said Mom standing in the doorway holding a tray, "We're all Corkers. 'out to astonish the *wor-r-rld*. After all that horseplay, you need a snack."

"Thanks, Mrs. R. My ancestors came from County Cork. I understand yours did too."

"We may even be first cousins."

"Katie, stop teasing, Brad. You know that isn't so, maybe second cousins."

"M-o-m, *stop that!*"

She winked at Brad and set the tray on my desk. "I'm off for choir practice. I know, Katie, that when I return, you'll have science in the bag. And, Katie, reel in those clothes, it looks like rain."

"Don't worry, Mrs. R., I'll keep her nose to the grindstone."

"I'm counting on you, Mr. S."

"Well, now that Mrs. R. has gone, is my tutor, Mr. S., *finally* ready to help me?"

"*Finally*, that's a laugh! Get out those books, Katie, me luv, less ye dither away the day."

"You'll not be blamin' me 'fer' that, Brad, me lad. Tutor, do *yer* duty."

Brad opened my science book but I couldn't concentrate. His voice hummed in the background. I thought about my first romance and the entanglement I might have gotten into. After Matt, I had concentrated on my studies and avoided dating. My mind wandered back to my diary and how Brad and I had first met.

Snap! Snap! I shook my head and stared blankly at Brad's snapping fingers when he said "Katie, you're miles away."

"Huh? Sorry, Brad. Read on, tutor."

"I *love* your enthusiasm, Katie. Do you want me to leave this for another day?"

"And miss this golden opportunity to be here *alone* with you?"

"Yeah, right! Come to think of it, that's not a bad idea."

Brad made a grab for me but I jumped off the bench and ran into the kitchen. He strode after me but I avoided his grasp and ran behind the island counter. Even his long arms couldn't reach me. He chased me around the counter. I grabbed a wet dishcloth and flung it at him. It landed in his mouth. I bolted for the front door and ran smack into Dad.

"Whoa, there. Katie! Where are you off too in such a hurry, and without your coat?"

"Dad, it's Brad. Protect me!" I laughed and hid behind him.

"If I know you, Katie Regan, Brad's probably the one who needs protecting."

"Hi, Mr. R. That girl of yours can't seem to buckle down to science. She's mighty distractin'."

"Just like her mother."

"Sure, gang up on me! Wait 'til Mom comes home, she'll set you straight."

"Where is she?"

"Choir practice," Brad and I answered in unison."

"That explains the shenanigans."

"Not entirely. Brad started the whole thing."

"Katie, stop ratting on me."

"Brad wouldn't give me my diary and then…"

"I can imagine," said Dad. "Gina had one of those too. It nearly drove me crazy. She finally let me read it after we were married."

"*Married!* By that time the pages will burn up with all the hot stuff Katie's written."

Dad laughed and said as he hung his coat in the closet, "She's a Corker, all right, Brad, just like her mom…nice flowers."

"Brad brought them."

"And on that note, Katie, me luv. I'll be takin' me leave. You must be tired after all that *studyin'*."

Dad went into the kitchen and Brad held my face in his hand. His eyes were full of mischief. My mouth parted for the sinking-in kiss I craved but instead of his mouth Brad plopped in the soggy dishcloth.

"Pthffth!" I spat. And before I could strike back, Brad grabbed both hands, kissed me on the top of my head, slapped me on my butt and escaped out the door and down the walk to the side of his orange Beetle. Still laughing, he mimed, *I'll call you.*

I put away my diary and re-read Grandmother Regan O'Neil's letter, more anxious than ever to explore her house, but the store was first on our agenda and I can hardly wait. I dwelled on Brad and our relationship. He looked surprised when Dad said that he didn't get to read Mom's diary until after they were married. Very embarrassing since Brad hadn't popped the question even though we had discussed a future together. I was still tingling from his kisses and the horseplay had stirred me up even more. I picked up my diary and read from the time Brad and I had started to date, two years ago.

Sadie Hawkins day approached and I still hadn't asked a guy for my date. All my friends were excited about going and I felt like a wallflower even though I was the one who had to do the asking. I moped around the house for weeks before the event until Dad probed for an answer. "Katie, are you sick? Are you having problems at school?"

I wailed, "I'm a wallflower."

At first he laughed but when I kept on sobbing Dad said, 'Katie, before you paste yourself to the wall like a drooping rose, your old Dad has a brainstorm. Why not ask Brad Shaughnessy? I went to school with his Dad, Clancy, and I know the family. Brad is home from Queen's for a few weeks preparing for exams. I'm sure he'll jump at the chance to have a date, especially with *my* beautiful daughter. I'll introduce him to you after Mass at the Autumn Fest.'

The meeting went better than I hoped. Our families hit it off, joking and reminiscing. Brad kidded his, soon-to-be married brother, Jack, as an old married man, and complimented Ruth, his fiancé, as looking like a child bride.

I couldn't keep my eyes off of Brad. He winked at me several times and finally he took my arm and said, 'Let's get away from all these old-married folks.' His easy-going manner dispelled my shyness and after we covered the normal questions about our schooling he surprised me when he said, 'I hope you haven't invited someone to the Sadie Hawkins dance. Katie. You don't want me to feel like a wallflower at my old Alma Mater, do you?'

Setup or not, I laughed and said, "No, I've been waiting for you to come home on semester."

"That's what I'd hoped. Oh, and. Katie, we wont stand on protocol. I'll pick up me Cinderella Sadie in me pumpkin." I was thrilled.

Brad wore my vegetable corsage and looked somewhat silly but mostly sexy as 'Li'l Abner.' I was none too warm in my 'Daisy Mae' costume with only a light cardigan. 'My chariot awaits,' he said and indicated his pumpkin, an orange Volkswagen Beetle. Brad carried me to his car, and the feelings I'd buried after Matt erupted all over again. I was smitten.

"Dad shouted from the doorway, 'What's a Shaughnessy doin' in an a pumpkin?'"

That was the beginning of our relationship.

I put my diary in the drawer and tidied my books. My hand touched Grandmother Regan O'Neil's letter. I patted then stuck it in my mirror. Her smiling reflection shadowed behind mine, and I was struck by our resemblance. She nodded and faded away leaving me more anxious to visit the little house she had willed to me. House, clothes, I almost forgot. I absently reeled in the clothesline. My mind was on Brad and the exciting events that had transpired. *That is funny*, my green bikini is missing and I don't see it anywhere.

6

Our great new venture, or as Dad had said, 'adventure', was about to begin. I could hardly wait to go inside. We stood beneath the faded sign, 'Regan's Hardware, Established—1939.'

"Well, this is it," said Dad, inserting the key into the heavy brass-trimmed lock.

We stepped onto a pine floor and flipped the light switch revealing six, cobweb-enshrouded light fixtures, suspended on long chains and reflecting two aisles of stock. A large counter holding an antique brass cash register guarded the door. We walked down the aisles amid neatly marked bins of screws, nuts, bolts and clamps of every conceivable size. Handsaws, Swede, cross cut and even a circular mill saw were displayed high up on the back wall above a shelf with metal cans and crocks of every description.

"Antiques?"

"To you, Katie, yes, but not to me, probably to your Mom though. She's at least two years younger than I am."

"Oh, you! There you go again, Greg. Forget those antiques. We've lots of work cut out for us if we're ever going to get this store in running order. We'll need professional cleaners," she said swiping her finger across a dusty shelf.

Camping equipment, Coleman stoves, kerosene lanterns and batteries, boating gear, buoys, anchors, ropes, paddles and even kapok life preservers, hung or leaned against the wall and Dad said, "Eric and his friends gathered milkweed fluff for sailor's life jackets in World War Two."

A workbench supported a grinder, vise and tools. Stacks of lumber, barrels, stovepipes and bins filled the storeroom behind the store.

"What's behind those double doors?"

Dad jerked his thumb toward them and said, "Loading ramp, Katie."

A small washroom fit under the stairs leading to the second floor. We mounted the narrow pine steps, took a sharp turn left and followed the hall to the back apartment.

"Well, this is it, the place where I grew up."

Knotty pine cupboards lined the west wall. A porcelain apron sink with drain board were under the window and at right angles two large appliances, a 1950 era Frigidaire and a well-used, four-burner, double-oven stove completed the kitchen space. A studio couch and an over-stuffed armchair occupied the sitting area at the end of the room, complete with pipe-stand on top of a small table and beside the chair, a chrome and onyx pedestal ashtray.

"My Dad's chair," said Dad. "No one was allowed to sit in it, not even Eric."

"I can't imagine anyone wanting to," said Mom.

"Phew, nor I! It still reeks after all these years."

"Oh, we wanted to. One day when Mom and Dad were busy in the store, Eric sat in that chair and bragged, 'He'll never know.' Dad's pipe dangled from his mouth. 'I'm Sean Gregory Regan.' Without warning, Eric struck a match to the pipe. He jumped up when we heard Mom's footsteps on the stairs and dropped the match in the chair."

"*I smell smoke!*" said your grandmother.

Eric caught red-handed with the pipe still in his hand tried to find the match in the smoldering seam. Boy! Did he get an old-fashioned licking? Dad wasn't much for the modern grounding.

He had said over Mom's protests, 'Doesn't teach them a damn thing, Emma.' Much to your grandmother's relief, I got away with a warning and a scolding from your grandfather who had said, 'I hope you've learned a lesson from your brother's foolishness.' I learned a lesson all right. After the near fire, I never wanted to have anything to do with that smelly business, cancerous too. That's what finally took your grandfather, lung cancer, years before his time," said Dad, wiping a tear from his cheek.

We retraced our steps and looked into a combination bath and storage room with porcelain fixtures including a claw-footed tub. The next door opened onto another long room divided by a screen. Dusty Hudson Bay blankets lay neatly at the bottom of that bed and the adjoining captain's bed near the east window. Drooping pennants reminded me of an old stage set.

"Eric and I slept here, me on the top bunk. It came in handy when I had Doug Watson for a sleepover. Your grandfather had denounced sleepovers as, 'Utter nonsense! This sleepover business is ridiculous! I don't want to look at a strange face over my porridge. Can't discuss business or worse still, I can't even give Emma a little peck. It just wouldn't be the same.' Dad continued, "Eric had a private sign between our sections, for my benefit of course. I slept on the top bunk where I could look into Eric's side. It was great fun aiming paper airplanes at him, while he was sleeping. I guess I was a bit of a pest…didn't like to be ignored."

Mom had been silent through most of the tour but she laughed and said, "And today, Greg, you're more than *a bit of a pest.*"

The other large room was mostly vacant except for a worn studio couch and a faded gray rug with garlands of roses. A few boxes were the only items on the top shelf of the closet. All rooms had large metal grates in the floors, a source of heat from wood, then coal from the Quebec stove below. Pipes angled across the store ceiling before a furnace had updated heating.

"I've heard stories about those grate covers," said Mom.

"Eric and I used to lift that cover and dangle our feet above the store ceiling. We weren't as quiet as we had thought and were mistaken in thinking that our little prank would go undetected. Dad used to say, 'Emma, those boys need more to do than to dangle their feet above the heads of our customers while I'm busy at the cash register.' He was a disciplinarian but had a sense of humor with us, but not the effusive banter and storytelling he shared with his patrons. Eric and I were sorting stock in the back aisle when we overheard your grandfather tell this story to a group of farmers from Orillia."

"I remember the time Seamus O'Toole complained of a toothache to old Doc MacDonald? They'd been drinking Irish whiskey in the driving shed out of sight of their womenfolk.

Chuckles emitted from the farmers and Dad went on with his story. 'They'd been there a spell and neither one was feeling any pain.'

'I tell you,' Doc, 'complained O'Toole, 'this blitherin' tooth will be me death.'

'Wish tooth ish it?'

'Thish un, right here,' said O'Toole pointing to his mouth.

'I can yank that 'un right here and now,' said Doc, bending over and peering at the offending tooth. "Sish right down on thish runnin' board and I'll do the job.' O'Toole sat on the running board while Doc reached for the pliers on the workbench. 'Firsh,' he said, 'I thing we both need another wee swig.' They passed the bottle and Doc instructed, pliers weaving back and forth,...' Jush need to brace my knee aginst the truck. Now, Seamus, wish tooth ish it?'

Seamus pointed to the offending tooth and Doc wove unsteadily before him. Doc braced his knee against the Ford. He yanked and nearly pulled O'Toole off the running board.

'Here!' Doc ordered extending the bottle. 'Take another wee swig. I'll have un too.' He struggled to maintain cordiality and stand upright.'

O'Toole grabbed the bottle and pulled a good swig, blood and all. Then he said, 'Ish still hurts! Doc, you pulled the wrong un, so you did!'

'No!'

'Tish so! I swear on me mither's grave,' "said O'Toole, shaking and pointing to his mouth. 'Ish thish un'.

Doc grabbed the pliers, wove unsteadily and dropped them in the dirt. He picked them up, wiped them on his trousers and explained to O'Tool, *'for sanishtashun'*. Doc wove, a blur before O'Toole's eyes, then suddenly became surly and demanded, 'Damn yer Irish hide, Seamus O'Toole, wish tooth? Damn it! Wish tooth?'

Seamus pointed to the tooth and Doc pulled so hard that he landed on his backside and lifted Seamus O'Toole right off of the running board. By that time Doc was so drunk that he didn't know how many teeth he had pulled. In a somber mood, he later confessed to his wife, 'That drunken fool kept saying, *'Not that one, this one,'* so I kept on pulling.'

"Humpf!' huffed Mrs. MacDonald, 'it looked like more than one fool came out of that shed, you drunken old sot. You even kept one of his teeth for the tooth fairy. I never want to hear that stupid story again.'

"Whenever Doc started that tale, Mrs. MacDonald went right out the door to Bingo, taking her women guests with her." Dad continued, "According to your grandfather's story, Doc still pulled the wrong tooth and they proceeded in their drunken fashion with O'Toole agreeing to yet another extraction."

"'Those farmers laughed so hard that I thought their sides would split. After they left your grandmother said, 'I fail to see the humor of those two stupid, old coots.' 'Ah, Emma,' said your grandfather, 'Just look at the funny side of it.' Then he slapped his knee and started to laugh all over again."

'I need a break,' she harrumphed and turned her back on him. She walked over to where we 'd been listening and whispered as she rounded on us, *'Shame on you for eaves droppin'.'*

'We didn't mean to eavesdrop,' said Eric. 'We got trapped behind the aisle and once the story started, we were afraid to come out.'

'Well,' she hissed, 'you can come with me, right now.' She called, 'Sean, I'm takin' the boys for ice cream.' "The doorbell tinkled our exit and that was that."

"Were those tales true, Dad?"

"One never knew. Those stories were very exaggerated. Doc pulled one tooth, then two and finally the tale said all of his teeth. Seamus would have been unconscious had he had all those supposed extractions."

We left at the silly tale and I said, "Grandma was right. Those guys were silly old coots."

Dad looked around. "That about does it for up here."

We trooped down stairs. Mom and I headed for the dish and glassware displays. Their beauty shone though the dust. Some were still in boxed sets. I ran my hand around the gold rim and over the pink magnolias on a dish pattern named 'Rhythm.' 'Water Lily' denoted a box of crystal, delicate to the touch.

"Remember these, Katie." Mom asked as she picked up a 'Corn Flower' vase. "Nona willed me what was left of her set. There's only one vase, so…"

"For your collection, right, Mom."

She grinned. I took it for yes and reached for a vase of orange Depression glass. Pink and blue from the same era were interesting but an only set of a black cream and sugar fascinated me. I held it to the light and dusted it. Shamrocks in bas relief made it unique.

"Katie, they must have your name on them."

"My name isn't on here," I said as I inspected the bottom of the pitcher.

"Gotcha! They are rare, Katie. What I meant was, I want you to have them."

"Mom thanks so much." I held them to me. "I'll treasure them always."

Dad popped his head around the corner and said, "Say, you two! Leave enough for the customers."

"But, Dad, these are priceless."

"And," said Mom, "Katie *should* have them."

Pyrex mixing bowls in all sizes and colors as well as two large crockery bowls from the forties occupied a top shelf.

"Mom, what's this?" I held up a double-handled wooden device with curved wires on the ends.

"That, Katie, is a pie lifter. Most households had one. Grandpa Veltri made ours. Aunt Janet has it, but I claim this one."

"I suppose, Mom," I held a double-handled device with two cups with holes in them, "this is for your antique collection."

"As a matter of fact, yes. Katie. Ricers were used for straining cooked vegetables, very useful for making baby food."

"Look, Mom." I held a box marked 'Vegetable Shredder'—1950. "Suction cups?"

"To attach to a table. That shredder and those meat grinders were hand operated. Electric appliances were a rarity for our household."

"I'm glad *I* don't live in the olden days. It'd take half a day to bake a cake."

"Baking, Katie, with hand-held beaters was often a family affair. We pitched in and baked a week's supply of cookies, pies and tarts."

"Katie, there were many compensations to *the olden days*, as you put it, right, Gina?"

"Checking up on us, again, eh, Dad?"

"No, Katie," he laughed, "but I agree with your Mom."

"It was a time of peace and family after World War Two, There was a saying, 'The family that prays together, stays together.' Most of our courtship was church orientated. We danced at C.Y.O., our young people's club in our church basement. We gave concerts and plays, even chartered a trip to Toronto."

"That we did and oh, Greg, those were wonderful years but it wasn't all fun though. Remember these 'L'attrapeur des Mouches,' mouse traps."

"EEUWEE!"

"I know, Katie. They give me the creeps too. Even Nona Veltri hated to set them. One time she caught a mouse by his ear. He squealed so loudly she let him go. 'Silly, woman.' your Grandpa said, 'That mouse will come right back in. You won't be so soft when he nibbles in your pie cupboard.'

"Fly papers were equally disgusting," said Dad. "How we hated those buzzing flies stuck in their death throes. Eric pulled the wings off one of the victims. Dad bawled him out."

"EEUWEE! EEUWEE! You're making me sick."

"I agree, Katie. I only saw him do it once. Dad yanked Eric by the ear and said, 'Experiment be damned, don't you ever do that again.' 'Gee,' Eric had said, 'It was only a dirty old fly.' 'And,' Dad had answered, 'All the more reason not to touch it as there are more humane ways of getting rid of pests.' "Dad was a paradox. I didn't see those fly papers as being humane either."

"Yuck! Those rat traps are even more disgusting."

"True, but necessary, Katie. Well, gang, I think we've had enough for today."

We went home full of optimism and talked over plans for the grand re-opening.

7

While waiting for best friends since elementary school, Tina and Siobhan, I reflected on the box of cards and greetings from many classmates from my stay in hospital. Their cards and notes had lipstick kisses and 'Get well soon. We love you, Katie. Everyone in school is praying for you.'

Reminders, that I am very lucky to have such good friends.

A separate box, scented with lavender, held Brad's cards and pressed flowers. He was the one I most wanted to see but I missed these girls too. Today would be my first outing with them, a short one as work at the store had left me exhausted.

The bus ride was short and we ran into the Oshawa Centre Mall anxious to shed our winter wear, anticipating a new outfit. We sighed with longing over the new spring styles.

Tina asked. "What do you think of this skirt, Katie? And, guys, is this color right for me?" She put a bright blue sweater under my chin and said, "This would be perfect with your eyes." Then she flushed suddenly stopped chattering and said, "I'm sorry, Katie, I just didn't think."

"Forget it, Tina."

Siobhan said, "Katie, you look a little pale. Maybe you should sit."

"I'm okay, but I'm pooped."

They had almost finished making their selections. I took a mild interest in their choices but couldn't get into choosing something for myself. Absently, I began to put the discarded clothing back on hangers. Glancing in the mirror, I had the illusion that my eyes had taken on a greener hue. My concentration wavered and suddenly I felt weak. I sat on the dressing room chair and said, "I. . . I can't choose anything today. I have to go home."

"We can shop another time," said Siobhan, "when you're feeling better."

Supported by Tina and Siobhan we took the short walk to the cashier's desk. She took one look at me and dialed a taxi. I was dropped off first, insisting that I could make it to our door. I went straight to my room and collapsed on my bed in stunned silence.

Mom followed into my room. "Katie, what's wrong? Hon, you look very pale."

I smiled, "Just tired, Mom. I overdid it a bit with the store this morning and O.C. this afternoon. I'll have to pace myself a little better, that's all."

"Stay there, Katie, and rest or better still have a sleep. You can have dinner later," She covered me. "She needs more rest, Greg, and so do I. Katie might want to stay home tomorrow and have Brad come another time."

"Katie, I feel it's my fault. I've been so pre-occupied with the store. I let you work too hard"

"No Dad, it's not that. I haven't been sleeping very well. I'll feel better after I rest."

***

I drifted off and once again, me spirit seemed to be on a flightless journey back to Ireland. I sat at the table in the small cottage. I had bolted the door against the buffeting wind. Candles flickered over the whitewashed walls and their flames danced and multiplied on the pewter ware. Warmth from the candles resembled the warmth when I had knelt in front of the votive candle on the Blessed Mother's' altar. I recited a prayer. "Please, God, give me strength to bear life's hardships and to do yer holy will." The stew tantalized me senses. The wind had died down and I heard scraping.

"Bang! Bang! Bang! OPEN UP, Missus O'Neil!"

I flew to the door, snagging me skirt on a rough spot on the bench. Daniel O'Malley, a robust man bent his head to clear the low lintel and deposited me Pat on the rug in front of the fire and ordered, "Help me undress him! Our dory hit a rock when landin' and Pat wuz thrown out. I nearly fell out meself, so I did. I grabbed his jacket when he bobbed up the second time. He's 'bout drowned."

I rushed to undress Patrick. He was dead weight. Had it not been for Daniel, I niver could've managed on me own, and me Pat surely would've died. Yer Pat? I questioned then ignored the inner voice and concentrated on restoring warmth to Patrick's bluish body. I toweled him down, modesty in front of Daniel forgotten in the urgency of the task.

"Better get that blood a-movin', Missus O'Neil," said Daniel. Then cooing to Pat like a baby, he implored, "C'mon there, boyo! C'mon! Gotta go fishin' 'efore those McCaffrey's rob the seas of what's rightfully ours. C'mon, Pat, me lad!"

I worked just as hard rubbin' Patrick's arms and chest and soon a little color came to his face. His eyes fluttered and he called, Emma! Emma!"

"I'm here, Patrick…tea? Yes, tea," I said, jumping up but Daniel cut me off.

"Whiskey! He needs somthin' stronger'n tea."

Patrick's eyes flew open. He said, "Glory be! Yer not Emma! Where's me Emma?"

***

Back in my bed, fully awake and shivering. I got up, closed my window and went into the kitchen where I sat, shaken to the core of my being.

"Good grief! What's the matter, Katie? You look like you've seen a ghost. You're shivering. Put on your housecoat and go back to bed, dear. I'll fix you a cup of green tea with ginger in it, just the way you like it."

I came to in a daze and was startled when Mom remarked, "Oh, dear, you have a snag in your nightgown. I hope you haven't been sleepwalking."

I was transfixed between the tear to my skirt in my dream and the reality of the tear in my nightgown. My mind struggled to dissemble my confusion and I wondered if I'd ever have another night's normal sleep as these nightmares leave me exhausted.

Mom took me out of my reverie when she said, "That darned chair!

50

I've been meaning to sand that sliver, or better yet, I'll throw it out. Are you ready to have dinner, Katie?"

I picked at my food, reluctant to go back to bed. We watched Raymond on T.V., and soon Dad was falling asleep in his chair and Mom was struggling to stay awake to keep me company.

Finally, I gave in too and went back to bed. I lay awake and watched the green iridescent hands work their way around to one o'clock, two, then three. I couldn't concentrate on my prayers. When, I felt my Grandmother's presence. I mumbled the Lord's Prayer and awoke anticipating the smell of coffee. I joined Mom at the kitchen table and we sat, elbows on table. hands holding our heads, half awake.

Dad joked, "What's this, Gina? Do I have to do *everything* around here? No response, eh? I guess *I'll* have to be the one to make coffee this morning." Then he did his usual attention getting antic of pouring a stream of filtered water to the coffee pot. Mom was half asleep and Dad, not getting her response, lowered the coffee pot and poured a longer stream. That finally got Mom's attention and she said, "Greg, you're such a showoff. It wont seem so funny when you have to wipe up. Greg. I think I'll stay home with Katie."

"I thought that choir couldn't do without you."

"I guess they'll have to. You can pray for both of us."

"Mom. go ahead with Dad. I'll be fine."

"I know dear. Events finally caught up with me. I'm unusually tired this morning."

"We all are but, I'll carry on and say extra prayers for you heathens. Perhaps Brad should come on another Sunday. You both need to rest."

"Sure, Dad."

I crawled into bed and tried to make sense of my confusing dreams. I was afraid to go back to sleep. My Grandmother's presence reappeared and she said the strangest thing.

***

"Too much, Katie. I should've been more intuitive. Rest me darlin' girl. You've had enough revelations for now."

***

A peace settled over me and I awoke around eleven thirty, feeling much better. I showered and dressed. Mom was in the kitchen. I wrapped my arms around her waist and said, "Mom, I'm sorry to cause you so much trouble."

"You're never a trouble to me, Katie."

"I'll phone Brad," I said, and ask him to make it another time."

"That won't be necessary, dear. I already confirmed that brunch was on. That's him now."

I hurried to embrace him then glanced back a little awkwardly toward the kitchen. Mom had her head in the fridge. Our passionate embrace sent my blood tingling and my head swirling as I clung to Brad with pounding heart.

"Now, that's a smacker, if ever I saw one!" said Dad advancing up the walk. "I hope you have one left for me," he continued, clamping Brad's arm affectionately, as he pulled me out of Brad's embrace and into his. Dad planted a kiss on my forehead, released me and headed for the kitchen saying, "And now it's Gina's turn, the lucky gal."

I rolled my eyes and exclaimed, *"Fathers!"*

"I know." Brad smiled, "I've two sisters, remember?"

Dad spun Mom around, gave her a resounding smack on her lips. She responded breathlessly. "Greg, you almost made me spill the juice! Behave yourself in front of the kids."

"What's that got to do with it? Besides, they *aren't* kids, or haven't you noticed? He ignored Mom's protests, turned toward us and winked. "Now that was a smacker!" He laughed and said."You've got too much of your mother in you, Gina, worry, worry, worry."

"Oh, pooh!" said Mom. "Everything's ready. Let's eat."

After brunch, Mom and Dad went out to the garden to check our tulips. They came in and Mom announced that they were going to Kingsway Nurseries to choose a magnolia tree for the front yard.

"Gina," Dad protested, "I thought magnolia trees were planted in the fall."

Mom gave Dad a nudge. *"And,* I also want to check out the spring stock."

Dad got the message and left reluctantly. I had the feeling that he didn't want to leave Brad and me alone in the house too long so I covered my embarrassment by saying, "Fathers!"

"Brad grinned and repeated what he said at the door. "Yes, Katie, I know. My dad acts the same about my sisters…*overprotective!"* He reached over, took my hand, looked into my eyes and said. "I think too much of you, Katie, to have anything premature happen in our relationship. I'll wait as long as we have to."

My eyes brimmed and tear drops fell onto my opened text. I blushed at the significance. Brad pecked my cheek, more like a father-daughter kiss. I glowed at his protectiveness and smiled.

We settled into science and what seemed like no time my parents announced their return, with "Greg, you were right. It's too soon to buy that magnolia tree."

For the next week, I studied hard with Brad and had little time to think about anything else. Exams were finally over as were worries about my standings. I got an A for English and two B pluses for history and science.

"Exceptionally good, Katie," said Mrs Borovsky. "You must have studied very hard to make up for all the time you lost."

"I had a wonderful tutor." I smiled remembering all the hours Brad and I had spent together. Dad stayed at the lumber company for the rest of the month. He had given three weeks notice.

When he explained the circumstances to his boss, Mr. Jensen had kidded him about being one of their competitors, and Dad had said, 'I don't think my store will be much competition.' Mr. Jensen said, 'You never know, Greg. I wish you the very best on your new venture. I'm sure you'll be very successful.'

"It seems strange," said Mom, "but I know we'll adjust."

Strange, I thought. You haven't a clue about strange and neither do I until Grandmother Regan O'Neil reveals more to me.

"Wont that be a surprise, Katie?" asked Mom.

"Huh, what surprise?"

"Katie! You really are in a different world."

"Just daydreaming, I'm looking forward to going to Grandma's house. I've been so busy trying to catch up with my studies and..."

"Yes," Dad interrupted. "And you've worked like a beaver. We're very proud of you."

"Don't forget Brad. I wouldn't have been able to catch up had it not been for his help."

"Brad deserves much credit," said Mom. "We'll have to do something nice for him."

"Yes, Gina. you're right. I can give him a job at the hardware sweeping floors."

"Da-a-d! You wouldn't!" The joke was on me when I saw the merriment in his eyes.

Bob's Professional Cleaners were hired. Siobhan and Tina had been bugging me to go with us. I had told them about our amazing discoveries and described Regan's Hardware Store as being more like a museum.

"No kidding?" Tina said.

Siobhan said "Katie, ask if we can help?"

"Sure," said Dad, "If they've nothing better to do for Easter break, they're on. I'll pay them the going rate. We need many workers."

"Why didn't your Dad ask *me* to help?" asked Brad. "I know my way around a hardware. I worked two summers at House and Home Lumber. I can *even* sweep floors."

I laughed at the joke and acknowledged that much of the stock had to be up-dated especially in the boating and camping equipment area. You probably could get David Berard to help you. He's had a lot of experience as camp councilor. There are old kapok life preservers and many other items from the forties and fifties," I said.

"No kidding?"

"That's what everyone says, Brad. No kidding."

8

I fell into bed exhausted, as I had been every night. My muddled dreams about Patrick in Ireland remain mysteries. I tossed and turned and again, I was transported.

***

Sea mists and the phantom specter, me Grandmother Regan O'Neil swirled together beckoning me into a maelstrom of mystery and back into the cottage.

"Yer not me wife," Patrick screamed. "I want me, Emma."

"I'm here, luv," I cooed trying to calm him.

"Pay no niver mind," ordered Daniel O'Malley. "He's tetched from his dunkin'. Here let me give'm a swig o' this here whiskey. Soon he'll be right as rain." Daniel grabbed the whiskey bottle. "As a matter o' fact, I be needin' one meself, that is, if you don't mind, Missus?"

"Go ahead," I heard meself say. "Chamomile tea will probably be better than whiskey for me Pat. Prop him in that chair by the hearth," I ordered. "Just give him a wee drop and then you can give him the tea while I fetch a basin of warm water for his poor feet."

I carried the basin. It wobbled and spilled warm water over my arm when I heard. "Easy, darlin', go back to bed."

***

Suddenly, *I was me*, back in my own room. My arm was wet and so were my sheets.

I sat up, alarmed. My clock's iridescent green hands indicated four o'clock. I turned on my nightlight. My empty water glass had tumbled to the floor. I crawled over the footboard, dragged the wet sheets and carried them to the hamper in the bathroom. I squinted against the nightlight and toweled my arm. "Too wet," I said. Still groggy, I took off my soaked nightgown and dropped it into the hamper. I was confused. I kept questioning, Ireland, Patrick, water, I'm all wet? How can I be wet from a dream? Oh, yes, I spilled my water. My head throbbed. Guided by my hand, I felt along the wall until I reached the linen closet. I opened the door.

***

"Top o' the mornin' to ye, darlin'."

***

Patrick of my dreams was sitting on a shelf in the linen closet, naked and green, a small leprechaun.

I must have fainted for the voice coming into my head was Dad's. "My poor little girl. My, darling, Katie."

"Greg, Phone 911 and Dr. MacLean. I think Katie's had a relapse." Sensation of loving hands reaching out to help me mingled with sirens. Once again, I was in a familiar place, *the hospital?* Why am I back in hospital? I tried to reason but nothing made sense and far off I heard someone say, "She's coming 'round."

My eyes fluttered and Mom blurred at the bottom of the bed. I was lying on a gurney, in emergency and she said, "Thank, God."

"PATRICK, GO AWAY! I don't want him here!" I whimpered then begged. "Please, please, Dad, tell him to go back. I never want to see him again."

"Back where, dear?" asked Mom.

"There's no Patrick here," said Dad. "Do you have a friend, Patrick?"

"Try to relax, dear," said the nurse.

Pressure on my arm tightened. *"NO, Patrick, Let go of me!* I wont come with you! Can't you see? I'm busy! *GET AWAY FROM ME!*Why don't you leave me *alone? No! No! I can't! I WONT!"*I tried to shake him free but realized it was the nurse.

56

"Try to hold still, Katie, so I can get an accurate reading. Doctor, her blood pressure is a little high and so is her pulse."

The doctor on call re-checked and said. "That's accurate, nurse. We had better send her up to 516 for her own doctors to check her. I remember her. She's the little gal who went through that terrible accident a few months ago and had a remarkable recovery. She seems delirious. Has she had these spells since her surgery?"

"She seems confused from time to time," I heard Mom explaining, "and she sometimes has a tendency to walk in her sleep."

I heard Patrick in my head say *'not really,'* but it was Mom speaking. Her water glass tipped. She must have gone for clean linen. She was laying naked on the hall floor."

"Um-hm! Katie, can you hear me? I'm Doctor Bridges. We'll take you for a little ride and your parents will see you in your room."

"R-oom?" I stammered. "What room? I want my own room! *I want to go home!* I don't need to be here anymore! Oh, Grandma, can't you see I need you?"

"Her grandmother died while Katie was in hospital. It was a terrible shock to all of us," said Dad.

Rolling and turning sensations jiggled and bumped me along the hall, in and out of an elevator, along another hall and finally a sharp turn into a bright room where the cheerful nurse said, "Here we are, dear."

Mom took my hand. "I'm here, Katie. Dr. MacLean will be here in a few minutes." My eyes fluttered awake and I asked for Dad. "He's gone for coffee. How do you feel, sweetheart?"

"Groggy. Why am I here? I don't want to be in hospital *ever again.*"

"Dear, Katie. You must have fainted. We found you naked in the hall. Don't worry, dear, your doctors are going to give you a thorough checking just to be sure."

"But, Mom, I'm fine, just tired...so very tired. I'm sorry to be so much trouble. I'm wearing you and Daddy out."

"I heard that," said Dad arriving with coffee. "I'm as robust as the day Gina and I married, right, Gina?"

"Sure, Greg." Mom laughed and added, "Whatever you say."

Dr. MacLean came through the door, grinned at their banter and said, "Umm, coffee smells good."

"I'll get some for you."

"No. Just kidding, I've had several cups." He gave a noncommittal, "Hmm-m" as he checked my pulse and blood pressure. "Now, Katie, for a look at your eyes." Dr. MacLean. examined my eyes and said, "Everything looks fine but just to be sure, Katie, I want you to have another MRI before you leave the hospital and I've asked Dr. Saheed to ask you a few questions. When I get the results, I want to see you in my office as soon as you are out. Check with my nurse as I usually operate mornings."

"What questions? *I'M NOT CRAZY!*"

"No such thing, Katie, but your parents said that you have been having disturbing dreams. Maybe Dr. Saheed can explain some of them to you."

I wondered. How can he explain my dreams when they don't make any sense to me? I know that Mom and Dad are concerned and didn't want to worry them so I agreed. I lay cocooned in a big tunnel, the MRI machine. It wasn't a new experience but for some reason I suddenly felt panicky. "I need. I need." I tried to say and then I heard Grandmother O'Neil and relaxed.

***

"Hush, dear girl. You need to be quiet and let the machine do its job. Yer parents need to know yer fine and you are. Be quiet and all will be well."

***

My consultation with Dr. Saheed and his questions did nothing to provide answers, as I was purposefully vague. Revelations about Grandmother Regan O'Neil's presence and my disturbing dreams would affect his clinical appraisal and cause further worry to my parents. My past sleep-walking excursions elicited a professional "Um-hmm!"

The death of Grandmother O'Neil sparked his interest. "Given your history; sleepwalking, the resulting trauma and recovery from your accident and losing your grandmother have caused you to be over stressed. Barring no difficulties from your MRI, as you've been under a most unusual amount of strain, I'll send your results to your doctor. The best advice I can give, Katie, is for you to ease up and try to put more fun back into your life. I detect a resilient Irish nature in you, Katie, and have the greatest respect for your progress that most assuredly came from your inner strength. Addressing your earlier concerns as expressed to your parents, the answer is *no, you are not crazy*, just overwhelmed by all the events. I wont need to see you again."

"Thanks, Dr. Saheed. You've been most helpful," I said, exiting his office. Phew! I'm glad that's over.

Released from hospital, I sank back into the car exhausted but relieved and listened to Michael Buble's CD. The music seeped into my being. I closed my eyes, my Grandmother Regan O'Neil's eyes. I felt her reassuring presence and slept until I felt wheels crunch on our driveway.

My stomach growled and my mind said eggs. I couldn't face food while in hospital. I tackled breakfast or I should say brunch with gusto under the relieved amusement of my parents. Appetite sated, drowsiness overcame me. "I'm going back to bed for a while."

"Of course, dear," said Mom. "We're all exhausted. I'm going to have a rest." She glanced at Dad who nodded and sighed as though he had been released from a great burden.

I slept until four o'clock in the afternoon. Twelve hours had elapsed from the time Patrick had appeared as a leprechaun in the linen closet. I didn't want to think about that and hurried past the closet door, willing the memory out of my mind.

"Surprise!" said Mom as I entered the kitchen. "You have a visitor."

Tulips waved above Mom's head. It looked like she had a new Easter bonnet ready to topple at any moment. Brad stepped from behind Mom and I flung myself at him, crushing some tulips and knocking him off balance.

"Whoa!" he said, grabbing the counter top. "What did you feed this girl, Mrs. Regan? She's frisky as a colt."

My exuberance was boundless. I felt completely reenergized by all the loving support, I held Brad close and rocked in happiness.

"I'll get a vase for the flowers," said Mom, "and, Brad, stay for dinner."

Brad accompanied me to Dr. MacLean's office the next afternoon and after examining my eyes, Dr. MacLean smiled and said, "Everything's normal, Katie, as are the results of your MRI. Your eyes have healed beautifully."

I batted my eyes at him. Then he laughed and said, "Katie, Katie, Your amazing sense of humor will get you *out of or into* countless difficulties."

"After all," I laughed, "I come by it honestly, Irish and Italian."

"I'm sure you do, Katie."

"But, Dr. MacLean. I really didn't have to see a *shrink*, I mean, a psychiatrist."

Regan's Hardware needed all hands but Dad was so overprotective about me lifting that I finally left him and went to help Mom. I tackled a few questionable gadgets. "Pot menders? Why would anyone mend pots, why not buy new ones?"

"In frugal depression years and later when metal was needed for World War Two, your Grandfather Veltri mended pots. And, this clothes whitener is bluing. Nona Veltri tied a square in cotton and swished it back and forth in the rinse water."

Bars of Sunlight laundry soap advertised as 'All Pure Extra Soapy' and, White Naphtha Soap, scrub boards, brushes, wooden clothes pegs, ironing boards and clotheslines were displayed in 'Wash Day Necessities.'

I held up a heavy iron stamped 'Taylor Forbes of Guelph.' "Doorstop?"

"Maybe now, Katie," laughed Mom, "before electricity, water was poured into the hole on top. Great Nona Veltri kept several of them on the go, replacing a cooled iron with a hot one. It was a long process."

"Mark another one for the famous, Gina Regan kitchen collection. And this biscuit box?"

"Let's see, this is an old one, 'MacFarlane Lane & Co., established in 1817.' No, I'll ask Brad to set it up on the display shelf. We're ready for our grand opening."

Easter week had been crazy with activity, both at the store and at church with choir practice for Mom and extraordinary ministerial duties for Dad. Triduum began on Holy Thursday and finished after Easter Saturday Vigil or after the last mass on Easter Sunday for those wishing to attend in the morning. We were all exhausted and excited about our new venture.

"No cooking for you tonight, Gina, my love. What'll it be gang, pizza or Chinese."

"Pizza," I said not giving the others a chance.

9

Again I was transported into that other world and into the persona of Grandmother Emma Regan O'Neil. I lay naked in our double bed in the cottage waiting for me husband, Patrick. It was dark except for the moon shining in the window and the green hands of the alarm clock on the candle shelf by the door to the main room. At eleven o'clock, I heard Patrick banking peat for the night.

Shivering in anticipation of the lovemaking that I knew was to come, I raised the coverlet and welcomed Patrick into me arms, tingling at his words, "Me darlin', Emma," he whispered as he buried his face in me neck. "Me very own, colleen."

"That tickles." I laughed.

His mouth enveloped mine and his tongue traced tingly patterns between me lips, me teeth and into me cheek pockets. Then he plunged his tongue into me mouth. We locked in an urgent erotic love dance. I wrapped me legs around him and drew his wetness into me. I gasped and groaned, rising to him with every thrust. Carried on a tide of love and emotion, me sensations mounted. Wave after wave of pleasure inundated me being into a tumultuous crescendo.

"Oh! Oh! Patrick, me darlin' love," I gasped.

"Me thinks, Emma, me darlin', if the timin' be right, we might get our son."

"Or, a wee colleen?"

Patrick's face suddenly took on a greenish hue and he shrank away from me, into the leprechaun of my linen closet.

***

"DEAR, GOD!" I screamed, "I was Katie, not Emma. *"GET AWAY FROM ME! GET AWAY! AWAY! AWAY!"* I pushed frantically at the covers.

"KATIE! KATIE!" yelled Mom. "Wake up, Katie." She continued to shake my arm and called, "Greg! Greg!"

Dad hurried into my room. The moon shone into my window. The green hands on my alarm clock on my dresser registered eleven. "My alarm clock!" I screamed. "Take it away! I hate that clock! Please, Please, take it away!"

Dad removed the clock and Mom said, "There, there, dear. You're having another bad dream."

"The bathroom, please, just give me a few minutes." The sudden wetness signaled the onset of the period I had been expecting. My cycle had become very irregular since my accident. I had been reassured that under the circumstances it was to be expected, but it was not so. Everything seemed out of time and place. I had a sense of losing myself. Where was Grandmother Regan O'Neil when I needed her?

We sat at the kitchen table sipping cocoa. Repelled by the memory of the dream, and the strong surges that coursed through me I was fascinated by an awakening sense of being a mature woman. Finally, I went back to bed. I tossed and turned for what seemed like hours before I finally entered that other time.

***

Patrick and I were ship bound for Canada. Patrick's near drownin' ended his fishin' days. His drinkin' and carousin' made village life unbearable. Canada would be a new start, away from all his old vices.

"We be hav'n a fine son in the new land," said Patrick, pattin' me growin' belly. "Just like yer foin husband, eh, Emma?" He laughed, slapping his knee at his joke.

Foin indeed, I thought but said, "That is, if you can mend yer carousin' ways, especially for our wee Babe, Patrick, me love."

***

I awoke Saturday morning, the dreams of the night before buried in my subconscious. I dressed quickly for the grand opening of Regan's Hardware. We rushed to the store for last minute preparations for what turned out to be a great party. Business would officially begin next Tuesday, but for now, it was time to celebrate.

Dad cut the green ribbon with an air of official aplomb accompanied by Morgan Duffy on the flute. Paddy Cauley banged away on the Irish Bodhran and the crowd followed us into the decorated store for refreshments. Brad and David Berard were there, of course, as were Siobhan and Tina, Clancy and his Shaughnessy clan, even some of Granddad Regan's old cronies.

The small downstairs washroom was occupied, so I took Tina and Siobhan past the cordoned off staircase to the upstairs. The girls had a quick tour but something lured me to the boxes on the closet shelf and we excitedly lifted them down. They were full of costumes so I said, "Let's try them on, no one will miss us."

"Maybe they're Halloween costumes," said Tina. She pulled the red ballet dress over her head. "I'll pretend I'm in 'The Nutcracker.' Siobhan, please zip up."

"At your service, Tina."

"Oh, look at this emerald satin!" The dress, richly trimmed in black velvet and gold braid was beautiful. I put it on, spun around and hugged its richness to me. Shivers ran down my arms. Hard-toed dancing shoes completed the Irish dancing costume. I tied the laces and magically, Irish tunes rang in my head and I began to dance. I had never taken lessons but the steps resonated loudly on the floor much to our amazement. Suddenly, I hopped and rose a few feet and levitated for what seemed like an eternity, but what had to have been a few seconds. I looked down at Tina's and Siobhan's astounded faces and then I was back, upright on the floor. I was stunned! Then I heard.

***

"There now, me, darlin', granddaughter, I always knew you had it in you."

***

"I didn't see that!" said Tina tearing off the red dress. "I've got to get out of here! This place is spooked!"

"Nor did I!" said Siobhan, who showed considerable more calm as she dropped the dress and stared at me as though she saw a ghost. "Katie! Do you realize what happened?"

"No! No! I don't! Please, please, don't tell anyone! *I would die!* They'd all think I'm crazy. I don't want to see that *shrink* ever again. Say, cross your heart and hope to die."

Siobhan grabbed one hand and Tina the other. We locked fingers and repeated the oath we had used as children, but today it was very significant and Tina and Siobhan seemed frozen to the spot as I flung costumes into boxes. Tina agreed with Siobhan and said, "Let's get out of this creepy place."

Mom met us as we were coming downstairs. "Oh, there you are, giving the girls a tour."

"Something like that," I said.

"Girls, Do you think we'll ever get the apartments up to their former rental condition?"

"I . . . I don't know, Mrs. Regan." Tina said and looked at me for an answer.

"I guess it has possibilities," answered Siobhan, helpfully, and I agreed saying, "Yes, lots of possibilities." Possibilities and more mysteries, like my green bikini that is still missing, even after a thorough search of the garden.

The guests were thinning out and after another exhausting day, we pitched in and quickly cleaned up party remnants Finally the last well-wisher had signed our guest book and gone with promises to patronize Regan's Hardware and we went home anticipating our venture.

10

Easter Sunday was a true celebration. Brad sat beside me in Mass. His ministerial duties at St. Mary's had taken place Saturday evening at the Easter Vigil. I glanced at his class ring securely wrapped in tape to keep it from falling off of my finger and sharp familiar tingles surged through me as Brad entwined his fingers in mine. Dad read the epistle and Mom sang with the choir, 'Jesus Christ Has Risen Today, Halleluiah!' Easter was a glorious celebration and when we left church, I proudly showed Brad's ring to Siobhan and Tina.

"*You're engaged!*"blurted Tina.

"Tina!" exclaimed Siobhan.

"Not!" I laughed. "Just a promise."

"A promise between *us,*"Brad cut in.

"That's *so* exciting," said Tina.

"It certainly is," said Siobhan, giving me a wink.

"We ran to Brad's Beetle and headed home for brunch where I showed Brad's ring to Mom, who said, "*Very nice.*"Dad hugged me and winked at Brad who was expected at his house for dinner, a rare time for the Shaughnessys to get together with Brad home from Queen's and his brother, Jack's family, visiting from Toronto.

"I haven't seen much of him," said Brad.

"No wonder," I teased, "You've spent so much time at the hardware when you do come home, I'm lucky if I see you at all."

"You little minx, Katie. "I spend my study weeks here. Why I don't know because you're, *so distractin'?*"

"I know," I said as we embraced on the front porch and he held me closer than ever. I was aware of his maleness against my stomach and suddenly I pulled away, weak at the knees and put my hand on the railing.

"Katie! What is it? Are you having another spell?"

"You could call it that," I said, quickly covering my embarrassment.

Brad joked, "I didn't think my kisses would have such an effect on you."

"They don't. I mean...I..."

"Hey! Are you trying to tell me I'm losing my touch?"

"Never." I said, "Not ever, just a little dizzy, that's all." I drew my feelings deep inside. The feelings I felt in my dream in the cottage with Patrick, the feelings that I had subconsciously buried, preventing them from entering into my consciousness, until now that I...now, what?

"Katie, honey." Brad's voice brought me back to the present. "You look pale. I'll take you back inside and phone you later. Okay?"

"I...I mean your kisses are quite overwhelming, that's all."

"That's all?" he laughed. "Well I'll just see about the *'that's all,'* with a repeat performance." Brad grabbed for me but I eluded his grasp, escaped into the house and closed the door.

I was laughing on the outside but I was more mystified than ever about my dreams with Patrick. I wondered how they affected my broiling feelings for Brad and our relationship, now. His arousal was exciting but fulfillment for us both was premature for our future life together.

Brad's ring was a promise and a precious secret, 'until I give you a real diamond, Katie.'

The first time I was sick to my stomach was at school a few weeks after my mystifying encounter with Patrick in my dream. Siobhan accompanied me to the washroom and said, "Maybe it's something you ate, Katie," as she passed me paper towels over the cubicle. "You'd better skip phys ed. and go home."

"I think you're right."

"You're early!" Mom said and added, "You look a little bloated. It's not unusual before menstruation."

"I had my period two weeks ago," I said, perplexed.

"No doubt, your whole system is upset from your accident," said Mom. "You'll feel better after you have rested."

I felt much better after I rested but then I was sick again after supper. Mom felt my forehead and insisted on taking my temperature. I was just as insistent that I was fine but I complied and opened my mouth for her affirmation that my temperature was normal.

The sickness repeated on a regular basis, and it became normal for me to quickly excuse myself and run for the bathroom to vomit. I flushed the toilet repeatedly trying to conceal the sounds emitting from my lost dinner. I stood at the sink and looked in the mirror. "It can't be! That last dream with Patrick was so real." I shook my head and scolded. "Don't be so stupid, Katie. You can't get pregnant from a dream!" I turned sideways and looked at my bloated stomach. It looked more like a bulge, a rounding, unfamiliar to my normal flatness. I yanked my T shirt over my jeans that suddenly seemed tighter than usual. Nonsense! Absolute nonsense! I've been eating like a horse and exercising too since my accident, trying to build myself back to normal. Have to watch those carbs, Katie girl, that's all.

A rap on the door and Mom's "Are you all right, dear," brought me back to reality and I returned to the table but passed on dessert.

Mom shot Dad a quick look when he said, "What, rhubarb pie is one of your favorites?"

My stomach rolled at the thought of dessert and I said, "No, thanks, but I'll have green tea, more settling. "

"Katie," said Dad, "You're not leveling with us. First, you eat like you're starving and now that you *are* putting on a little weight, you head for the bathroom right after dinner. Then we hear flush after flush."

"My goodness, Greg!" Mom said then she turned to me and asked,

"Honey, I understand, you think you're gaining too much weight, don't you? I felt like that when I was your age."

"Huh, no!"

"Perhaps, it's something a little more serious," said Dad. "Could it be bulimia? All that toilet flushing every time after you eat dinner is a sign that all isn't quite well with you, dear."

"Maybe your school health councilor has some ideas that would help, Katie," said Mom.

"Sure, sure, you're probably right. I'll ask her tomorrow."

Pamphlet's—'Your Child and Eating Disorders—Anorexia nervosa and Bulimia nervosa,' 'Cause and Effects' were spread before me. I was positive that I had no eating disorder but, *something*, must be wrong with my system.

Brad had a special surprise for my birthday. He took me to Anthony's Restaurant for dinner. Unfortunately, my after-dinner-sickness repeated in the cramped restaurant washroom and when I came out of the cubicle my retching elicited a remark from a concerned patron washing her hands. I nodded when she asked if I was okay and she nearly blew me away when she said,

"Don't worry, dear. I was like that for the first three months and then my morning sickness disappeared. I never had any with my next pregnancy."

I left the bathroom in a daze and barely found my way back to our table where Brad waited, anxious to settle into 'Black Forest Cake,' and when I said we had to leave, he looked shocked and said, "Leave, but dessert, don't you even want…?" He stopped mid sentence, grabbed my jacket and draped it over my shoulders. He threw fifty bucks on the table and said to the startled waitress approaching with coffee, "Keep the change."

Brad bundled me into the car and we drove home in silence. "Katie," he asked when we pulled up in front of my house, "Is there something you want to tell me...anything at all?"

"No," I said, "I can't right now...later. I'll tell you later." I gave him a quick peck on the cheek, ready to bolt out the door but he clasped me to him and asked, "Are you sure, sweet? You can tell old Brad. Who loves you more than I do?"

"Nobody," I sniffed.

"I hope not. You seem a little out of sorts, that's all. Maybe you should see your doctor."

"*Doctor?*"

"Yes, Katie, doctor. You're probably run down from that darned accident." He slapped the steering wheel with the palm of his hand, "*All my fault.*"

"Brad, Brad! Stop blaming yourself!"

"I know," he said, "but if I hadn't let you ride that darned motorcycle in the first place you never would have ridden past that house. I love you so much, Katie. I can't see a future without you. I don't want *anything else* to happen to you."

"I know, Brad, and I'll be fine. Thank God for my eye bank donor. I can see but there's more. I've been sick to my stomach for the last few weeks, mostly after supper, and I don't know why. It worries me."

"My point exactly, Katie. You need to have a good check-up and probably a boost of B vitamins."

"I...I guess," I smiled limply and turned my cheek as I felt anything but appetizing. He'll never understand about my Grandmother's presence, my strange dreams and how they affect me. I'll lose him for sure just like I had lost Matt. I put on a brave front, one that I didn't feel, and said, "Everythin' will work out, dearie."

"So, it's, dearie, is it? All of a sudden, I'm dearie?"

"Oops, sorry, Brad. All of a sudden, I'm sounding like Grandmother O'Neil."

"Katie, You never *met* your Grandmother O'Neil."

"Not in this life," I said.

"Katie, have you been throwing salt over your shoulder? I didn't think you were superstitious."

"No, no, I'm not. It's just…just that she's been on my mind so much lately, that's all. Her will, leaving her house to me and getting Regan's Hardware ready for the opening. We haven't even gone to her house yet."

"Another new venture?" asked Brad.

"It really looks like it will be, maybe it will help solve some mysteries."

Brad walked me to the door, held me in his arms and went to kiss me on the mouth. "*Wha*-a-at, wha-a-at's this?" He asked in an exaggerated Irish accent.

I pulled away and teased, "I'll take all the kisses you offer when I freshen up. C'mon in."

"What's this, home early?' asked Mom. "No dancing at the Jubilee?"

"We decided to neck in the car instead," I quipped and headed for the bathroom.

"Yeah," laughed Brad. "We can always dance."

"I'm also sure, even with the dance that you can get in a little necking on the side," teased Dad.

"Greg." said Mom.

"I heard that." I yelled from behind the closed bathroom door and then there was an awkward silence until Dad said, "Brad, could I have a word with you…outside?"

I returned to the room and shot Mom and inquiring look.

"Sure, Mr. Regan," said Brad and then he said to me. "I'll be back in a minute, Katie."

The minute became two, then three. Then I heard Brad's outburst beyond the front door. "I don't give a damn *what you think of me* but *I do give a damn what you think about Katie*, for God's sake, she's *your only daughter*! You should damn well be ashamed of yourself! Tell Katie…Never mind, I'll tell her myself…later."

His car door slammed, the engine revved and with a screech of brakes, Brad was gone.

"He's gone!" I yelled at Dad. *"It's your fault!* What did *you* say to him?"

"Calm down, Katie." Dad said walking toward me. "Calm down, Hon."

"GET AWAY FROM ME! I wont calm down after what you just did! Don't call me, Hon, either! I'm not your honey and *I never will be again!"*

"Gina?" Dad asked, appealing to Mom.

"You're on your own with this one, Greg, you and your temper, always jumping to conclusions."

"WHAT CONCLUSIONS?" I screamed.

"It's just that we've been struggling to help you, Katie," appealed Dad.

"SOME HELP!" I screamed. "I don't need anymore of *YOUR HELP! I LOVE BRAD!* If we have any differences, we can work them out."

"I certainly hope so," said Dad. "I certainly hope so."

"What's that supposed to mean, you certainly hope so," I countered. *"That and your conclusions."* I started to cry.

"Greg," tempered Mom, sensing the escalation. "Katie deserves an explanation."

"I think Katie's the one who has some explaining to do," said Dad. "If she's pregnant we certainly have the right to know. She's only seventeen and it's our responsibility to protect her, even if she can't protect herself."

"We already discussed that possibility," said Mom.

"THE BOTH OF YOU! *PREGNANT? YOU THINK I'M PREGNANT!"* I fled to my room and buried my sobs in my pillow.

"Katie, Katie," called Mom knocking on my bedroom door.

"GO AWAY! I don't want to see either of you! Just go away!" I cried myself asleep and again entered into my Emma O'Neil state.

11

Patrick and I disembarked from the ship with our pathetic bundles. The crossing from Ireland had been hard on me and I was glad to find an upstairs room, all that we could afford, in a shabby rooming house in St. John, New Brunswick.

We weren't settled when Patrick announced. "Emma, this place is stifling. I can't take the confinement after such a long journey. You rest and I'll take a wee walk about town with Jake MacNamara? You mind, we met on the ship."

"Yes, Patrick. I know, too well, about that good-for-nothin' drunkard! You promised me you'd quit yer drinkin' when we got to Canada."

"Aw, Emma, c'mon. What's a little drink between friends? It cheers me up."

"Yes, and it cheers me down, Patrick. Yer not yer happy self when you drink. You think yer the life of the party and a barrel o' laughs, a drunkard's illusion, that's what you have."

"Sure, I be the life of the party."

"Sure and yer not, and what's more, Patrick, yer not the great lover you think you be, either. Remember that poor O'Hara girl back in Ireland, carrying yer babe."

"Now, now, Emma. You've been listnin' to all that washerwomen talk. Just a bunch of gossipin' old women, that's all."

"Yer not about to fool me, Patrick O'Neil. Yer name was blathered all over, and not just with that O'Hara girl, either. What about Maggie Cassidy?" I knew it was useless but I asked anyway. "Explain her away if you can."

"Gossip, just ugly gossip," was Patrick's feeble defense. "Probably started by Daniel O'Malley. He always was jealous of me way with the colleens."

"Shame on you, Patrick O'Neil! Him yer best friend. Even saved yer life. Fer

shame! Go! Go on with you then! Get out of me sight, Yer upsettin' our babe! He's doin' a jig in me belly."

"Have it yer way," he shouted as he went out and slammed the door.

I suddenly felt faint and sat down on the floor with terrible cramps and a wetness between me legs! It seeped into me skirt! I screamed, "Patrick! Patrick, For the love of God, Patrick, Come back!"

Patrick's boots clamored down the stairs and out into the night.

"Dear God!" I screamed. "I've lost me babe! Help me! Please, help me!"

***

"Katie! Katie! Mom burst into my room and threw the light switch. "Oh, Katie! Our darling girl! God, please help us! Greg, Call 911! Tell them to page Dr. Giometti. I think. . .I think Katie's had a miscarriage."

Dad stood in the doorway, too shocked to move until Mom shouted at him again.

"Me babe. Me poor wee babe," I whimpered, caught between my dream and the scenario taking place around me."

"GREG, SNAP OUT OF IT!" Mom shouted through my subconscious, "Call our doctor."

Dr. Giometti lived within blocks of us and arrived in minutes. Mom helped me and I sat in a daze on the toilet. Dr. Giometti went straight to me, took my pulse and blood pressure and ordered Mom to take me back to bed. He examined the bloodied sheets and said, "No miscarriage here, just a normal, but rather heavy menstruation. When her period is over, bring her in for a complete pelvic. And *you, young lady*, stay in bed for the day. You need more rest, probably all that activity helping out in the hardware didn't help, either." He gave Dad a meaningful look. "That and the accident, no doubt, have upset her whole system."

Mom removed the sheets and my nightgown from the bathtub and took them to the laundry. I watched, too furious by their accusations to speak to them. I took a warm bath.

In the morning I refused breakfast. I skipped school and disdaining our kitchen telephone, sent Brad a text message. NEED YOU LOVE K.

I flew into Brad's arms, sobbing, before he reached our door. "Please, Brad, Get me out of here! I can't take any more."

Brad glanced nervously at Mom, standing at the sink and within earshot of my passionate plea. Tears streamed down her face and she said, "Go ahead, Brad. Katie needs you right now. Take her away for a while."

He nodded to Mom and said, "C'mon, Katie. We'll walk to 'Mike's Fish Restaurant.' The fresh air will do you good." He wrapped his arm over my shoulder and when we reached Mike's, Brad headed for the back where we sat opposite each other, concealed by the booth where he said, "I'm starving, What about you?"

"I'm hungry too, Brad, but first, I have so much to tell you." I swallowed a gulp of water before I began and noted Brad's worried expression. "Mom and Dad thought I was bulimic and that's why I visited Nurse Jacobs' office. I was developing a fullness I couldn't explain. Then my parents thought I was pregnant. I love you so much, Brad. It might be too easy for me to be careless and spoil everything but I wouldn't do that. You know, 'Catholic girls don't' is the credo in our family, but we both know, Catholic girls sometimes do and are just as apt to get pregnant, too late for regrets, but..." Brad reached over and covered my hand with his. "Please, Brad. This is hard enough. Let me go on. My parents know I am in love with you and they are worried about my increased fervor for you."

"I know," said Brad. "Your Dad had a talk with me that day at your house. I was so mad I wanted to sock him. He knows how close we've become, and being a father he sensed my passion and love for you. I want you so badly Katie. I swing between passion and frustration and know we'll be happier in the long run if we wait until we're married, even if it almost kills me."

"Oh, Brad! I love you so. I'm sorry. I don't want to frustrate you. I'm frustrated too and I've been having so many confusing nightmares."

"I sense your anxiety too Katie. I don't know about *your* nightmares but I have dreams that I'll loose you if I let myself get out of control. That's why I've decided to go away for the summer. I've accepted a job at 'Deerhurst Lodge.' It'll give us a chance to cool down. Next year, I'll graduate, get a permanent job and then we'll be able to realize our dreams."

"Oh, Brad!" Tears rolled down my cheeks. "I'm so glad that you'll be here for a while. I need you so much. Would you come with me to Grandmother Regan O'Neil's house? I haven't been there yet and I'd rather go with you than with Mom and Dad. Right now. I need some space away from them. I know they're exhausted with worry over me but I'm being smothered by their concern. I'm so angry and hurt by their suspicions."

"Of course, I'll go with you, Katie. I'll always stand by you. Surely you must know that."

"I know, Brad. It's just that I'm so frightened. My dreams are perplexing."

Brad got up, sat beside me, encircled me in his arms and said, "I'm here, Katie, right here. Tell old Brad what's troubling you. After all, dreams are only dreams."

I grinned at the 'old Brad' part and said, "But, Brad, you don't understand. My dreams are so real. In them I'm me, but I'm someone else too, like I'm two people."

"Sometimes I feel like that too. Sometimes I'm a student with an upcoming summer job at 'Deerhurst,' and at other times, my hormones take over and I just want to marry you and make love to you."

"Brad, I feel like that too, but it's not quite like that for me. In my dreams, I *am* my Grandmother O'Neil, and I think like and answer to Emma. In my dreams, I *am* married to her first husband, Patrick, and it's very real even his lovemaking." My dreams have aroused feelings I had never felt before and I don't want to have them with that Patrick.

"Oh!" I gasped aloud overwhelmed by the stimulating emotions. Brad quirked an eyebrow and I blushed. It was as though I had drawn Brad into me in my desperation. The same feelings I had felt in my dream had resurfaced, and I suddenly felt weak and regretted what I had just revealed, repulsed that I had let Patrick make love to me. But it wasn't *me*. I was Emma.

"Hey, there, Katie!" Brad gave me a gentle shake, "I know I'm a potent mixture of virility and charm but..."

"Brad, stop! You don't understand!"

"Help me then, Katie. Just *help* me." Brad looked a little disappointed, as though his charm and virility had no affect on me.

"I'm trying, Brad. I'm really trying. It's just that...Brad, I was pregnant."

"My God, Katie! What are you saying? How is it possible, after all we both said and how much we mean to each other?"

"Darling, Brad," I began.

"Don't, darling, Brad me, Katie. I need more than your sympathy and your platitudes." He pulled his arm from my shoulder and shook my hand away from his.

"Brad! *Not for real*, Brad! *In my dreams, I was pregnant in my dreams* when I was Emma married to her first husband, Patrick. I lost the baby, Emma and Patrick's baby. Patrick went out drinking and left me alone. I called to him to come back but he left me. All I heard were my screams and his boots echoing down the stairs. That was when I awoke screaming, 'Me babe. I lost me babe.' My period had flooded the bedding and I was screaming and screaming."

"Oh, God, Katie!" Brad enfolded me in the awkward confines of the booth. "Your Grandmother O'Neil, the will?"

"Yes, Brad. My Grandmother O'Neil came to me in the hospital."

"But, Katie," Brad protested. "How could that be? Your Grandmother was dead when you were in hospital."

"She came, Brad! I really met her! I floated above my bed. Mom said the doctors thought they had lost me. It happened twice while I was in hospital."

"Twice?"

"Yes, Brad. The first time was right after the accident. I hovered above my body and saw this old woman. She was leaning over me and crying. I didn't know then that she was my Grandmother the one I had never met or even seen her picture."

"*That* old woman?" asked Brad.

"Yes, Brad. *That* old woman had been the crossing guard at St. Paul's. Do you remember the time you pushed your way to the front of the line?"

"I wanted to be beside a little girl, Katie Regan. I nearly pushed you off of the curb."

"Yes, only you did push me off the curb," I laughed.

"I remember it all," said Brad. "The crossing guard saved you from that passing car."

"That's right, Brad. She was Grandmother O'Neil. She explained everything. I was a preemie in hospital. She saw my birth announcement in the paper and volunteered as rocking granny so she could see me and get a chance to hold me, which she did, but only once. Mom and Dad had taken me home and when she came back, I was gone. I felt so sorry for her. I felt her presence then and sometimes she comes back to me. She is the grandmother I never knew. I finally saw her picture among those included in the album after we read the will."

"Katie, you're giving me goose bumps!"

"If you think you have goose bumps, wait until I tell you about Patrick. Patrick turned into a leprechaun in my dream. Then I woke up. In another dream, I spilled warm water from a basin. I awoke with a start and found that I had knocked my glass of water onto my arm. The water soaked my sheets and nightgown. I got up, threw the sheets and my nightgown in the hamper and went to the hall closet to get more sheets. It was then that I saw him." I shuddered.

"Who did you see, Katie? You look like you're going to faint. Take a deep breath and a sip of water. That's better. Now, who did you see?"

"I saw Patrick sitting on the shelf. Only he was small and green like a leprechaun. I fainted and awoke in the hospital. They thought I was crazy. I never told Dr. Saheed, the psychiatrist, or he would've really thought so too."

"Katie, dear Katie, this whole thing is bizarre; your grandmother's eyes, your dreams, Patrick, a leprechaun? Katie, your imagination has run away with you! Your closeness to the grandmother you never met has stirred up all these feelings, something like transference. I don't know if that's the proper term but you seem to have related so much to your Grandmother Regan O'Neil because of the loss you feel in never knowing her. It looks like you not only want to know her, but your empathy is so great, that at times you even feel like *you are her.*"

"Maybe…I guess, but, Brad, if you would come with me to her house, these feelings of disconnectedness that keep returning may be resolved."

"I certainly hope so. *Of course,* I'll come with you. I'll always support you. Circumstances have mounted against you, confusing circumstances. Have you told your parents all this?"

"No! I've already caused them so much worry. You saw Mom this morning. She could barely speak. I couldn't conceive getting pregnant from a dream but all the signs were there. Dr. Giometti wants me to come in for a pelvic examination to make sure I'm okay. I'm so nervous, I can't carry on alone. Brad, please come with me."

"Of course I'll come with you, Katie. We're in this together, all the way, remember?"

"Yes, all the way. I remember, Brad."

"I've come to a decision," said Brad.

"About…?"

"I've decided not to go to 'Deerhurst' this summer. I'm going to stay right here and work at Regan's Hardware. I'll see *you, us,* through this, Katie, my girl." Then he started to sing, 'K…K…Katie.'"

"Oh, Brad, you've made me feel better and you always make me laugh."

After my pelvic examination, Dr. Giometti's said, "Well, Katie, my dear. Your worries are groundless. You are a perfectly normal seventeen year-old, perhaps a little more mature than your parents are willing to acknowledge. You were not pregnant as I said at the house. Your hymen is intact. You *are* a virgin. I suspect you long for marriage and a family."

I sniffled. "I knew I wasn't pregnant, Dr. Giometti. I've had so many confusing dreams since my accident."

"There, there, dear," he said smiling and patting my knee reassuringly. "You know, Katie. sometimes women who are traumatized or very much want to have a family experience the same symptoms as if they were pregnant. I've seen it happen to a patient who was in her forties. She felt her time-clock ticking. She wanted to be pregnant so badly that she believed she was. She experienced morning sickness, swelling and a cessation of her menses. It does happen. Yes, Dear, it does happen. So you see, Katie, enjoy your wonderful life. When you plan and wait, Dear, good things will come your way including a family that you seem to want so badly. Enjoy each day, no need to rush."

"Thank you. Doctor," I said. and thought. Thanks for the relief, not for the embarrassment.

"That-a-girl," he said. "Now get dressed and go out and reassure your boyfriend. He is a fine chap to accompany you here."

Brad and I hurriedly exited the waiting room. Brad bought us lunch at the Tim Horton kiosk in the hospital and we took it to the park bench where I related my ordeal.

"Poor, baby, I'll bet you're glad that's over?"

"It was such an embarrassment, Brad, mostly for what my parents thought about me."

On the drive home, Brad asked, "You're going to tell your Mom now, aren't you, Katie? She was crying when we left."

"I will, Brad, but I'm still angry at them for thinking I was pregnant."

"I know, Katie, but even you had your doubts. You've been through a terrible ordeal and they have too. You'll all feel better, as I did, when they know the whole story."

Mom looked expectantly when we came into the house. I cried, flew into her arms, clung to her and said, "Mom, oh, Mom, I'm so sorry." I passed her a tea towel and retrieved it to wipe my tears. "Please sit down, Mom, and I'll make a pot of ginger tea. I have so much to tell you."

"I'll make the tea," announced Brad, "and what's this, wiping your faces with a tea towel? Didn't your mothers ever tell you 'That's a no, no?'"

Mom sat silently while I related the events that had been troubling me. Then she said, "My darling, daughter. I'm so sorry we doubted you. Your Dad has been distraught for days. He'll be so relieved. It was just that you were getting better and then all of a sudden…"

"I know…"

Brad said, "Wham!"

"What's this?" Dad said, pausing at the door.

"Good news!" I blurted and flew into his arms knocking him against the closed door.

"And now," I announced. "I'm going to Grandmother Regan O'Neil's house."

"But, Katie. You've been through so much and…"

Mom interrupted and said, "Greg, this is something Katie needs to do *without us*. Besides, Brad will be with her. You will go with her, wont you, Brad?"

12

As Brad's 'Beetle' approached Grandmother Regan O'Neil's house, *my house*, my heart beat in fear of what the small, south facing house would reveal. A peek-roofed porch with iron railings protected the front door centered between two windows. I fumbled the keys and finally passed them to Brad. We stepped into a small room, more like a vestibule than a living room and looked around. I stared transfixed. Emotions swirled through me and I started to shake.

"Are you all right, Katie?" Brad asked, putting his hands on my shoulders.

"Huh? Yes...I guess. It's just that...I don't know how to explain it."

"You don't have to explain it, Hon. You've done enough explaining for one day. We don't have to see everything at once. We can always come back. We can go whenever you want to"

"I'm fine," Brad, "I said reassuringly," but, I had a sixth sense that all was not well here.

The bookcase to the right of the door served as a tabletop for the settee on the west wall. An armchair with a large sewing basket in front and a tall floor-come-table-lamp completed the cozy corner. Truly, this was Grandmother Regan O'Neil's chair where I was drawn. I ran my hand over the crocheted doilies covering the arms and back. I felt her calm presence dispelling my earlier trepidations. Windows above the settee cast light into the room and reflected onto the opposite wall where a small T.V. stood between two open doorways. One was the bathroom complete with a claw-footed-tub.

I said, "Brad. I'll save grandmother's room for last."

The kitchen was equipped with fifties-style-appliances. A kitchen door and narrow stairs led to the cellar. Brad reached over me and switched on the light. Jars of preserves, fruit and pickles, lined one wall. Pottery crocks and a barrel of dishes faced the stairs. Curious, I took a piece of china from the top of the barrel and unwrapped the yellowed newspaper. The markings on the delicate tea plate were so fragile that when I held the cream porcelain piece up to the light, I could see the shadow of my fingers. It was 'Belleek,' an Irish porcelain plate embossed with delicate tracings and green shamrocks.

"Oh, Brad! Look at this!"

"It really is beautiful but I think we'd better look at the rest of the house. You do want to see the back yard in daylight, don't you, Katie?"

The oil furnace clicked on and we climbed the stairs, passed through the kitchen and into the sunroom behind the living room. An afghan-covered daybed and a chest of drawers lit by a lamp completed the space.

We continued our tour into the small garden. Only a few tulips remained on their stems, their blooms reflecting the receding light. Most of the petals had fallen to the ground. Purple and yellow budding iris and overhanging branches of lilac showed promise of a beautiful display. A bed of roses, not yet in bloom encircled the back half of a small pool. A mischievous leprechaun guarded the pool.

"That's the first thing I'll get rid of," I said with a shudder.

"Katie," said Brad. "I thought you loved leprechauns. Most Irish do. You know, *'fairies,'* little people and all that."

"Not me! It's a silly Irish superstition. Lets go back inside and check out my grandmother's bedroom."

Brad slipped into the bathroom and I entered her bedroom. Garden scenes covered walls and made the small place seem even smaller, yet cozy. The handmade quilt, of a log cabin design, covered the double bed. I ran my hand over the many patches arranged and crafted by my grandmother, scraps from used clothing made into this beautiful work of art. White pillows decorated with crocheted roses propped against the iron headboard. A small rag doll, curled into a fetal position, rested between the pillows. *'Me, babe, me poor lost babe,'* echoed from deep within.

I plunked on her bed and stared at my reflection in the mirror. There were two reflections. She materialized and her wispy presence sat down beside me and I gasped, "Grandmother! Where have you been? I needed you so...Patrick...my dreams."

"To whom are you speaking?" Brad stood in the bedroom doorway. His face drained of all color. He stared at Grandmother Regan O'Neil.

***

"It's all right, me Boyo," she said. *"You've naught to fear."*

***

Brad grabbed my arm and yanked me off the bed. *"KATIE, LET'S GO!"*

***

"Stay for a wee while."

***

She said this as though she was inviting us for tea and biscuits.

"I...we..." Brad stammered.

"It's okay, Brad. It's the way I told you."

"I don't understand," said Brad *"and I don't want to understand. I don't believe it."*

I tried to reassure him. "Brad, please, it's okay, but my grandmother spoke again.

***

"Mind yer manners now, Boyo. I'm not an it, nor was I iver one."

***

"I'm sorry...very sorry. It's just that..." Brad's voice trailed off.

***

"I know, me Boyo, I'm just an illusion, but, a good one, eh? I'm glad yer here with Katie. I've a score to settle with a master illusionist. He knows who he be."

84

***

"Pa...Patrick?"

***

"That's right, dearie, Patrick, me iver lovin', Patrick. The man of me dreams, the love of me life. He hurt me beyond measure with his womanizin' and drinkin'. I forgave him many times even with that O'Hara girl and Maggie Cassidy when they had his babes. I thought he'd change when we came to Canada but that was not the case. He caused me to lose our babe. He denied it all. 'Damn, gossipin', washerwomen.' That's all he'd say even when his best friend, Daniel O'Malley, who saved his life, said it was so. 'Just lies,' was all he'd iver say. He left me for sure and by the time he returned, if he iver did, I wuz taken, by the grace of God, to the good nuns who cared for me. But for them I would've died."

***

Suddenly, the Patrick of my nightmares and the bothersome vagrant to our families appeared as a vaporous leprechaun. He snatched the shillelagh from the umbrellas stand in the corner and brandished it like a sword.

I fell back against Brad who tried to ease me toward the door but the power of the illusion was so great we were rooted to the spot.

***

"A curse on you, Emma O'Neil, for yer damn lies. You deserve another beatin' with me shillelagh. It seems like I be the one with a score to settle, Emma, me, iver lovin', wife, loosin' our babe like you did. Emma, me darlin', it's all yer fault. You lost me son. You put a hex on the babe and had a colleen but it really was me son, me real son, Sean O'Neil. When you thought I'd drowned you went to Oshawa and married Sean Regan. You really put it to me, Emma, marryin' a Sean."

***

I held onto Brad in rigid fear and shook so badly I thought I'd levitate right through the roof and take Brad with me but it was not to be. I watched in horror as the scene unfolded.

***

"You SILLY OLD COOT!" screamed Grandmother O'Neil. "Yer just as daft in yer illusion as you be in the flesh. Git away, with you! You'll niver beat me agin or anyone else for that matter. Yer illusions don't scare me."

***

"You don't know all there be about the afterlife, Emma, me foin wife. I'll settle this once and fer all, with yer precious granddaughter," challenged Patrick. "I be havin' the powers and I have Katie. Tis not you I be after, you old witch."

***

Patrick or his illusion grabbed the shillelagh, raised his green arm and swung it toward me, but my grandmother's image stood between us.

***

"Not so fast, Patrick, me luv. "There be a greater power than yer old tricks and God is on our side. May He preserve yer soul."

***

Grandmother's image stood its ground protecting us from Patrick's illusion, his gnarled finger pointing at us. Brad grabbed me by both arms and shoved me. He grabbed the doorknob.

***

"Not so fast, me foin colleen."

***

"Not so fast, YERSELF, Patrick, yer blarney-mouthed drunkard!" Grandmother screamed. "Patrick, you may have had the best of me in the past but this be yer last hurrah. Niver you mind," she nodded at us, "God be with us!"

***

Patrick, the leprechaun, raised the shillelagh, but it was wrenched from his grasp and into the hands of my grandmother's presence.

***

"For the Glory of God and all His Saints, be gone with you and all yer tricks, Patrick, and don't you iver bother with us again. BE GONE WITH YOU!"

***

She raised her arm and pointed the shillelagh at the crucifix. Suddenly the plastic image of Christ seemed to illuminate and vibrate on the wall and come away from the cross toward us. A feeling of peace settled over me when in my heart I felt, '*It's finished.* 'Patrick who had looked like the green red-eyed leprechaun in the garden seemed to turn into an insidious iridescent vapor and evaporated into a thin-green wisp exiting through the keyhole.

***

"Katie, me darlin', I thought I could change Patrick's ways and exorcise him out of me mind on me own. Me pride got the best of me. Me job here appears to be finished. Enjoy yer little house and when yer time comes, I'm sure you'll be in hiven 'efore the devil knows yer dead. Praise the Lord."

***

Brad and I made the sign of the cross and gazed at the crucifix on the wall and the shillelagh in the umbrella stand. Vanishing rays cast shadows across the porch as we silently locked the door and said in unison, "The Lord, be praised."

PART TWO

13

Brad has completed his degree in chemistry at Queen's and I took advertising design at the Ontario College of Art. Over three years have passed since my near fatal accident on Mr. Shaughnessy's 'Indian Motorcycle.' My eyes have completely healed, thanks to the generosity of Grandmother Regan O'Neil's who gifted her eyes to the eye bank. She died of a heart attack when she saw my inert body on the snow after the explosion.

Brad and I have been living in the little house she willed to me since we were married last August. The same house that I first entered with so much trepidation, the house where the culmination of my many disturbing dreams about Patrick and Ireland ended when the illusion of Patrick's spirit was vanquished out of my dreams and out of our house, forever.

Marriage and waiting for Brad's has been more than I had ever dreamed, as he is very loving and so much fun. I was a little worried about our wedding night as I had heard a few unsettling stories that the first time for the bride, especially if she's a virgin, isn't that pleasant but Brad's teasing started at our reception and never let up.

He had carried me over the threshold and into the kitchen. I had made a funny face at him and had asked, "Why the kitchen?"

"Because, Katie, me foin young bride, 'twould bring me shame to be givin' the tusslin' you've been waitin' fer without feedin' yer face." He sat me down, and said, "Ta da!" and produced the confection bride and groom from the top of our cake. "Now this is how 'tis done. I'll go first."

He took the confection bride, kissed her face then licked her from top to bottom and wiggled his tongue on her feet. Then said, "Now it's your turn." I laughed so hard I nearly fell over. "This is serious," he said. His eyes twinkled. He was anything but. "Here, Katie, let me help." He passed the groom to me and shoved its face onto my lips.

"All right, all right, Brad, you silly goose. I'll do it. I copied Brad's licking actions without taking my eyes from his. "Okay, I'm done."

Brad shook his head no. Then he kissed the bride confection on her breasts, her privates then turned her over and kissed her bum. I blushed at the implication but was so aroused I couldn't think. He pressed the groom confection to me and I imitated his play.

"That was just for appetizers, Katie, me bride. The best is yet to come." He scooped me up, and carried me into the bedroom and said, "First, we'll play strip tease. Then, we'll play doctor. I'll be the doctor." Brad did another "Ta da!" and with each succeeding 'Ta da, he took off another item of my clothing and kissed me on the spot he had uncovered and encouraged me to mimic his actions. "C'mon, Katie, me love! Get with the program." Encouraged by my fun-loving, wonderful man, who I've loved all these years, my shyness left and he lifted me to an exquisite peak of pleasure where we have traveled many times.

Now we are expecting our first child in May of 2000. I don't want to know if it's a colleen or a lad. Either, to us, will be God's blessing.

Gina Regan, my mom, is so looking forward to her first grandchild. She has been knitting a storm in anticipation of the blessed event and fussing over me as though I was an invalid. She has been like that ever since the explosion and the resulting traumas I suffered afterwards. I know I would be the same if I was in her shoes but I do wish she'd lighten up. Her fussing has become contagious as Brad and my Dad have become mega-fussers, and I've been fussing over house work. I want everything to be perfect when our baby comes so I've been on a mad house-cleaning spree. Yesterday, I had a few cramps when I reached to clean the top cupboard. It was the last shelf, and then the kitchen cleaning would be finished so I ignored the cramp and chalked it up to a bit too much stretching until I awoke in the night screaming.

"Brad! Brad! Wake up, Brad! Wake Up! I think my water broke!"

"Wha...what?" Brad mumbled in a sleepy fog.

"Brad, my baby! It's too soon! Dear God, help my poor baby! Grandmother O'Neil where are you? Help!" My screams of panic seemed like they were coming from some place far away, as was Brad's voice shouting into the phone.

Another gush of amniotic fluid pushed me into a higher level of panic and I screamed, "Towels, Brad, for God's sake, hurry! It's too soon! Our baby will die! Dear God, *please help us!*"

***

"Hush, dear child," said the presence of my grandmother. "I'm hiven-sent to help with yer babe the same as I was drawn to become a rockin' granny when you were a preemie, as they were called."

***

"Grandmother O'Neil, where have you been these past years?"

***

"I be here now, child. Try to be calm for the baby's sake. A worrisome birth but you'll be fine and so will yer babe. Now, take some deep breaths and say the Lord's Prayer together."

***

A calm settled over me. The ambulance attendants arrived with a gurney and I heard one say, "Fred, the room's too small to maneuver the gurney, help me lift her."

"I'll lift her," said Brad, picking me up covers and all and lowering me gently onto the gurney.

"Don't you worry now, little mother," said Fred as he bundled me up and tied me onto the gurney. "Rick and I have delivered a lot of babies. We'll be at the hospital before you know it."

Their confidence was reassuring. They carried me down the front steps. It was snowing and snowflakes landed on my face, 'angels kisses.' I worried, "Where's Brad? I need, Brad!"

Once in the ambulance Fred said, "Don't worry, dear, your husband can ride up front with Michelle. She's an excellent driver. We'll be at the hospital before you know it."

In spite of the efforts of Dr. Giometti, my gynecologist, he was unable to prolong my pregnancy. My screams denying an early birth were useless and Emma Angela Shaughnessy was born Mar 17, 2000. I felt her loss to my womb, until she was placed on my stomach. I reached down and touched her wet squirming warmth until the nurse took her to wash and weigh. My preemie at five and a half pounds was a very good weight, affirmed Dr. Giometti, for a baby born midway through my last trimester.

Tears of relief and joy overwhelmed me. I smiled then cried silently into Brad's shoulder.

The nurse carried Emma Angela and asked Brad. "Would you like to hold your little bundle?"

Brad adjusted his hospital gown and awkwardly held out his arms for our baby. His eyes brimmed as he snuggled her little head under his chin and held her awkwardly. His hand took up most of her little body.

I giggled and said, "Brad, you look just like the picture of my Grandfather Regan when he held his first born, Eric, like you're holding a ham, or a turkey."

The nurse grinned and said, "All new fathers hold their babies like that. Here, let me show you. That's right. One hand always supports baby's head. Newborns are pretty wobbly but strong and they sometimes turn unexpectedly."

Brad adjusted Emma Angela into the nape of his neck and nuzzled her head into his face. He took a deep breath as though drawing her exquisite new baby smells into him.

My emotions were overwhelmingly mixed as I wanted to snatch my baby from him, My baby that Dr. Giometti had recently placed on my stomach right after her birth, but she was our baby and the filial love of father and daughter in their first bonding, held me back. Finally, Brad bent down and lay Emma Angela in my arms, kissing the top of her head as he did so. He kissed me his tears falling on my face. "Thank you, my darling, Katie."

"Thank, God!" I said. "And thank Grandmother O'Neil."

"Grandmother O'Neil?"

"Yes. Brad, my Grandmother O'Neil. She came to me when I was giving birth and told me not to fear and that she was heaven-sent to help me. We said the Lord's Prayer and a calm overcame me, as before, you know, Brad?"

Brad raised an eyebrow, gave a sigh and said, "Yes, Katie, I know. I'm grateful for whatever peace you find. You know that."

Brad's comment 'for whatever peace you find' perplexed me. He was right there in our house, in her room with her spirit when the power of Christ on the crucifix expelled Patrick's presence as a leprechaun, out of the house and out of our lives forever. We even had Father Byrne bless our house before we moved in.

We were ecstatic holding our first born, this child of God's and our love was miraculous. I forgot about Brad's comment as I felt Emma Angela's little heart beat against my breast. Tears of thanksgiving rolled down my cheeks and onto her downy hair. Brad bent over and wiped my face then his own.

Our joy was subdued, as the woman in the bed behind the curtain had lost her baby. The nurse shook her head sadly when she revealed the poor woman had suffered her third loss, a previous birth and her husband who had died in an automobile accident. We were even more grateful for our good fortune.

Our parents had been anxiously waiting. They had arrived at the hospital before four in the morning. They were considerably subdued, knowing about the woman's circumstances. My parents were the first to visit. Their tired faces lit up with controlled joy and awe as they beheld our little angel.

"Oh, Katie!" Mom breathed a sigh of relief. "Thank, God! She's so perfect."

"Just like her mother," said Brad.

"Yes, Brad, almost as perfect as her mother," said Dad. Then he laughed and said, "Once a Corker, always a Corker."

"Greg," scolded Mom. Brad gave him a look. We grinned when we realized it was Dad's little joke. Mom was itching to hold Emma Angela. She had donned a gown for that very purpose. I reluctantly opened my arms for her to take our baby from her position over my heart. Again, I felt the impulse to snatch her back and scolded. Don't be so silly, Katie, or you'll be like your parents, overprotective.

Then it was Dad's turn. He held Emma Angela as an experienced teary-eyed grandfather. He reluctantly passed her back to Brad and said, "Gina, we'd better give the Shaughnessys a turn. Clancy's been pacing the halls with me for what seemed like hours. They'll be anxious to see you, Katie, and the baby."

Brad passed Emma Angela to his mom. She and Mr. Schaughnessy wore gowns. Brad's dad wore a mask as he had recently recovered from a cold and explained that he didn't want to take any chances. Brad's mom, Marie, 'O-o-o-d' and 'Aw-ed,' the same as my parents had and his dad made clicking sounds in Emma Angela's direction. She arched her little neck toward the clicking with cross-eyed concentration.

"She smiled!" Brad's dad said. "She smiled at me! I bet I'm the first person she smiled at."

"Dear, Clancy," said Marie. "She probably just had a little bubble of gas."

Brad's dad looked disappointed. "No, Marie. She smiled at me. See, she did it again!"

"You're right, Dad," Brad said. "See, Mom, Katie, she did it again."

"That was a smile," said Marie, passing Emma Angela back to me.

"I agree, a smile from an Irish colleen to her Irish grandfather."

"I have to go too, Katie, as I have to buy a car seat for our baby. After all, our little angel flew down to us a few weeks ahead of schedule."

"And I'm going with him." said Mom, "to get a few more things for the baby."

The nurse came back and said, "You need to rest now, Katie. You've had quite a few visitors. The grandparents will be delighted to see you at home"

"Home, already! She was just born a few hours ago!"

"I know, dear, hospital policy. Dr. Giometti has recommended you stay an extra day. You'll be going home Sunday noon. It does seem a little soon, dear, but it's far better than it was for mothers in the 1950's and earlier. Those poor mothers were often kept abed for ten days or more. When they finally got up, some of them were so weak they could hardly stand. Many had to return home and care for large families. Some mothers even had multiple births like the quintuplets of Corbeil, Ontario. They were put on display in Calendar."

"I remember Mom talking about them. Nona Veltri visited Calendar and saw the Dionne quintuplets. The 'Quints,' as they were called, were separated from their siblings at birth and were cared for by Dr. Dafoe who became famous for delivering them. My grandmother had bought souvenir hankies with pictures of the babies printed on them for mom and her sister. My grandmother also had a small picture of the Dionne home."

The nurse said, "Emily died in nineteen hundred and fifty four and Marie died in nineteen hundred and seventy. Their births attracted much publicity, capitalized by 'the Province of Ontario.' to help sell War Bonds. Annette, Cecile and Yvonne collected four million Canadian dollars on March six, nineteen hundred and ninety-eight. Yvonne died in two thousand and one. a heartbreaking situation for all."

"I'd be heartbroken if I had to part with my dear little baby."

"You've nothing to fear with your loving husband and her doting grandparents."

"I'm very blessed but right now my breasts are full and uncomfortable and my baby is trying to nurse."

"Here, dear, let me help you," said the nurse. "That's right cuddle her under your arm and put her face on your breast. Her little mouth will instinctively search for your nipple. Your milk will come in a few days. In the meantime, protein rich colostrums will secrete for several days. It will help to give your baby a good start."

Drops of colostrums seeped from my breasts and I helped Emma Angela's little mouth find my nipple. She nursed naturally. Varying sensations of joy mixed with a slight discomfort in my uterus caused me to moan,

The nurse gave a knowing smile and said encouragingly, "I'm aware of all the sensations you are feeling, dear. I felt them too as do most mothers. They are all very natural. Your baby looks like she has a lusty appetite. She'll be fine, you both will be."

Emma Angela sighed and relaxed her mouth from my nipple. Tiny droplets of pearly colostrums dripped into her open mouth. I sat her between my legs, the way the nurse showed me, and held her little chin with one hand and patted her back with the other.

"That's right, dear," she encouraged. "Premature babies sometimes have reflux and it saves getting burble down your back."

Emma Angela nursed every few hours much to my relief as my breasts ached. I was comforted by Grandmother Regan O'Neil's appearance.

***

"There now, Dearie. You have a fine colleen. Thanks, be to God."

***

I said, "Amen!"

The woman in the bed next to mine went home today. I prayed for her and for her loss and was all the more grateful for our many blessings and for those of the mothers whose babies I viewed through the nursery window.

Brad arrived with clothes for both of us, his nervous twitch replaced with a grin plastered all over his face when he said, "Our family."

I had just finished burping Emma Angel and the nurse came in to help us get ready for home and our big adventure. I protested when she ordered me into a wheelchair and with brisk efficiency said, "I'll carry your little bundle and Daddy can push Mommy."

Brad pushed the wheelchair with one hand and held his bouquet of roses in the other. My overnight bag was on my lap and I carried the plants from our parents. Our new car seat passed inspection and Emma Angela was strapped backwards for safety regulations. We drove home on this beautiful sunny day. A day that seemed most appropriate, as March, nineteen was the Feast of St. Joseph, patron saint of families and of Canada. Brad drove with extra caution and we were home within fifteen minutes.

Brad said, "Katie, I'll help you up the stairs first, then I'll come back for our baby."

"No, Brad!" Someone may steal her!"

"No one is going to steal your baby," said Dad already at our car. "Brad, I'll help Katie and you bring Emma Angela."

Dad had shoveled the walk. Mom waited inside where everything was in readiness. She had helped Brad set up Emma's temporary bed on top of the dresser, the bottom of the Lloyd's baby carriage that Nona Veltri had used for her in the seventies plus two top drawers filled with baby needs. She and Dad had bought a dresser and set it up in the bathroom. "'For the time being,'

Mom had said. "You can use the top for a change table, Katie."

Now, she greeted. "Come dears, and sit down, lunch is ready."

"Mom, you think of everything. We're so grateful for all your help."

"Brad, you must be starving," said Mom"

"What about me? Don't grandfather's count?"

"Greg," Mom laughed, "you always count. You know that but today you're second."

Brad had taken our baby out of her bunting bag and brought her to me to nurse.

"Hmm," Dad asked, "Don't you think you'll be more comfortable nursing in the bedroom?"

I laughed. "Dad! Where have you been? Don't you remember all those mothers protesting on T.V. over their right to nurse in public?"

"Greg, don't be so old fashioned," said Mom. "After all, we are family."

I snuggled Emma Angela to my breast and pulled the light blanket almost covering her head in deference to Dad when Brad said, "Katie, don't cover her. I want to take your pictures."

"But, Brad, I look awful…my hair."

"Hush, Katie," said Mom.

Dad said, "Brad, take their pictures. They'll never be more beautiful."

My protests were ignored and later, when Brad placed our picture on our bedroom wall beside the crucifix, I joked and said in an exaggerated Irish accent. "Wh-a-a-t s this, not in our living room above Grandmother Regan O'Neil's chair?"

Now our pictures grace two walls.

It is hard to believe that four years had gone since Brad gave me his class ring and we made our first promise to each other. Fun filled years when even bringing in the groceries could erupt into horseplay. Like the time Brad threw one orange after the other at me at such a pace that before I could catch the next one the kitchen floor was covered in oranges.

Spring was a good time to have a baby. Awkwardness in handling Emma Angela was temporary and I soon settled into a routine. She went to Mass with us where I could nurse her in the choir loft. I sang along with Mom and the other choir members. Emma Angela cooed and waved her little hands and kicked her feet to the beat of the music. Soon Lent will culminate when Christ's Resurrection is celebrated at Saturday, Easter Vigil Mass.

Easter Sunday dinner at Shaughnessys' was a reunion with Brad's brother, Jack and his wife, Ruth and their children, Shanna, age two, and four year-old, Ronny. Brad's sisters were with their in-laws. Easter egg hunt excitement was over and we gathered in the living room.

"Picture time," Jack said. "I want to get Emma Angela's picture with Shanna and Ronny holding her."

"First," said Ruth as she scooped up Shanna "Come to the kitchen with me, young lady and I'll take that Easter bunny off your face."

"No! No! I wanna keep bunny."

"You can keep your Easter bunny, my little bumpkin," said Ruth. "I just want to wash the chocolate off your face and hands."

"No! I not bumpkin!" Then the defiant little miss changed, as though a light switched on and said, "Shanna wanna hold baby."

The cousins wiggled their little bottoms on the chesterfield and pushed each other for the best spot. I leaned down and held Emma Angela closer to them and said, "Emma, this is your cousin, Shanna," I took Emma's little hand and stretched it out for Shanna to take. Suddenly, Shanna grabbed Emma's hand in both of hers and almost pulled her out of my grasp. "Easy, dear, I'll let you hold her in a minute, after I introduce her to Ronny."

Emma gave a big yawn and Ronny shouted, "Aunt Katie! You've gotta send her back! She's not finished! God forgot her teeth!"

We laughed and I asked, "Would you like to hold your toothless baby cousin? I'll sit in the middle and you each can sit beside me."

It had been a wonderful day but Emma started to fuss and I was glad to return home.

14

Brad returned as Technician in Nuclear Medicine and I settled into a comfortable routine with Emma Angela. I no longer wanted to postpone taking her to the garden as most snowdrops had gone. I walked along the path and directed Emma's little hands explaining as I went. "These yellow flowers are daffodils, and these are tulips. See, they are starting to bud." Emma cooed, as I talked to her in a singsong voice. I continued and waved. "We'll have beautiful blooms of purple and white lilacs and, precious, our roses will bud like your sweet rosebud mouth."

Emma waved her arms and kicked her feet. Suddenly she stopped and stared, as though transfixed, at the leprechaun by the garden pond. She became very quiet. I followed her gaze and gasped. "NO, NO, NOT AGAIN! NOT WITH MY BABY!" My eyes played tricks on me."

***

'Tis a trick all right, Katie. Get back in the house and bolt the door!"

***

Shivers ran down my spine. I clutched Emma to me and ran for the house. I bolted the door, grabbed my cell and sent a message. BRAD! TROUBLE! I snatched the crucifix off the wall, placed it at Emma's back and shakily sang, "Hush, little baby, don't you cry."

***

"There there, hush now, Katie," said Grandmother O'Neil's presence. "Say the Lord's Prayer with me."

***

Brad stood speechless in the doorway. I knew he saw Grandmother O'Neil when he looked from her to me.

***

"You can pray a bit too, Brad. Don't you think?"

***

My shaking stopped and Brad, gently took the crucifix and hung it up. Dear God, what does it mean? Emma Angela gave a beatific look at the crucifix and then she smiled at the misty presence. She nuzzled my breast and I lay down on the bed and held her over my pounding heart.

One day when Brad was at work, I answered a knock at our front door and a stranger said, "Missus, it looks like yer hedge be needin' a clippin.' I've been out of work fer a spell. I be stayin' at Shady Elms and need a bit o' cash. I don't charge much…just need a little cash to wet me whistle."

I slid the safety chain across the door and looked at him through the small opening and stammered, "I…huh. My husband does all the yard work. He's been a little busy lately."

Emma chose that moment to fuss and the stranger said, "Ah, ye have a wee babe. Would it be a lad or a colleen, fair as the mother I almost see through the crack in the door?"

There was something about him…that crooked smile and a somewhat familiar Irish accent.

"A baby girl." Instantly, I regretted that I had indulged him with an answer.

"Ah, a wee colleen. I was supposed to have a son once, but she put a hex on me and had a colleen instead."

I slammed the door, threw both safety bolts and ran to our bedroom. Emma still fussed but first I grabbed my cell phone and sent a text. BRAD HOME TROUBLE! I latched the cellar door and later wondered why as it had no access from the outside. I heard him at the sun porch door. He peered through the curtains with his hands cupped around his eyes. I bolted that door and yanked on the blind covering the door. The blind snapped and revealed Patrick, the same Patrick from my nightmares in Ireland. The very one, who's image as a vaporous leprechaun was banished from this house and out of our lives forever. "Dear God, how can this be happening?"

I tried to reassure myself. This cannot be. Patrick's dead! He must have a brother. Yet, I saw him with my very eyes. He is the Patrick of my dreams but much older. I struggled to control my fear as I ran back to our bedroom, snatched Emma from her crib and clutched her to me, fearing for our future in this house.

Brad arrived within minutes and I almost hyperventilated in disbelief as I gasped out my fears, "Brad, Brad! It was *him*, Patrick! I saw him at our door!"

"Katie, Katie, get a grip on yourself, you'll scare the baby! Here, blow into this. I've called your mother. She'll be here any minute."

He put a paper bag up to my face and I began to breathe, in and out, in and out. Everything turned pink and I slumped forward. When I came to Mom had placed a cold washcloth on my head and Dr. Giometti came in the door.

"She's been under a lot of strain," said Dr. Giometti as he felt my pulse. He put the blood pressure cuff on my arm and I lapsed into the fear of my dreams and screamed. "No, No! Patrick, Let go of my arm! I wont come with you, ever again! *Go away* from me, Patrick, Go Away!" The blood pressure cuff triggered the same reaction as I had had in hospital after I saw Patrick as a leprechaun in my closet.

"Patrick?" asked Dr. Giometti. "Who's Patrick?"

"No, Doctor! No! Not Brad's cousin, Brad knows that! I mean the Patrick of my nightmares, *that Patrick.*" I pleaded trying to make them understand. "Brad, tell Dr. Giometti!"

Brad startled me when he shouted, "FOR THE LOVE OF GOD, KATIE! Get a grip on yourself! You'll scare the baby!"

Dr. Giometti looked at Brad, sharply. Brad's face reddened and the doctor turned to me. "Tell me what happened to upset you so, dear Katie."

I started to cry. "A man came to our door. Brad, you must have seen him, he just left! You must have seen someone. Brad, I'm trying to tell you that the man at our door looked like the Patrick of my nightmares. He even sounded like him. He said he needed work and wanted to trim our hedge. When he heard Emma fuss, he asked if she was a colleen or a boy. Then he said a startling thing. 'Ah, a wee colleen, I was supposed to have a son once but she put a hex on me and had a colleen instead.'" I shook in the retelling and Brad suddenly turned pale. He sat down beside me and frowned.

"Come to think of it, a poorly dressed guy wearing a Blue Jays' cap and a flash of green from his pocket was waiting at the Garrard Road bus stop. It struck me as an incongruous getup. Was he wearing a baseball cap?"

"That's him, Brad. Oh, Brad, call the police. I never want to see him again. He said he stays at Shady Elms on Simcoe Street South."

"Don't worry, Katie. We'll look after everything, won't we Dr. Giometti?"

"Yes, Katie," he said, and his kind brown eyes gave me a sense of surety.

I shook my head to dispel the thoughts I had verbalized. I wish I could erase the words that caused my mother to collapse on the chair and Brad's forehead to crease in worry.

"You know, Katie," said Dr. Giometti. "You've been under an unusual amount of trauma in your short life. It isn't unusual for new mothers, particularly mothers who have premature babies, to suffer post partum stress. Your chart indicates you confided in Dr. Saheed a few years back. He's a good man and very understanding. He looked at Brad who stood staring in open-mouthed disbelief.

"No, no! I'm not crazy! It's because…it's because in my dreams, my nightmares, that man looked like the same man. He scared me, that's all."

"There, there, dear," said Dr. Giometti, as he kindly patted me on the arm. "You must be calm for your baby's sake. Upsets often cause mother's milk to change and your baby will be the first to react."

"I'm sorry, Dr. Giometti. I'll try not to worry and I will go and talk to Dr. Saheed, if you think that will help."

"Yes, I do, and I also think that you need full time help for a while. You've been under too much stress and it's not good to be left alone with one's thoughts. I hesitate to give a prescription to a nursing mom. Perhaps you will find a glass of warm milk will have a calming effect, Katie," he added patting my shoulder.

"I'll fix some," said Mom. "Would you care to have tea with us, Dr. Giometti?"

"Thanks, but no, Mrs. Regan. I have another mother due at any time and I want to catch a few hours rest."

Brad set up trays in the living room. I sat on the couch "He was real, Brad. He really looked like the Patrick of my nightmares."

Brad bit his lip. "Don't worry, Katie. I'll look into it. He'll never come back here to bother you whoever he is."

"Who was real, dear?" Mom asked coming from the kitchen.

Brad glanced at her and shook his head.

Brad, don't dismiss my concerns as though they are insignificant."

"Katie, you know I'll look into it. Please, don't worry. Doctor's orders."

15

Brad decided not to call the police, for the time being, but to do a little investigating on his own. He entered Shady Elms halfway house and went into a large room, identified by a sign at the entrance as' Common Room.' A small group fixated their gaze on 'The Simpson's,' and didn't bother to look up. Four men were playing cards and Brad's presence caught the attention of one of the players.

"Hi, Dude," greeted the younger one with spiked hair, nose and earrings. "Lookin' for someone?"

"Yes, as a matter of fact," said Brad. "A guy with an Irish accent came to my house looking for work."

The gray-haired guy with the ponytail looked up and said, "Oh, you must mean Jake, Jake MacNamara. I think he's out back, holdin' court with someone. Just follow the hall." He jerked his thumb indicating the direction.

Brad said, "Thanks" and went out the back door. Two guys were sitting under an elm tree laughing, apparently having a great time.

"Jake, you're a Corker. Tell me another one," said the listener.

"Now stop me if ye heard it 'efore," said Jake.

Brad stood in the doorway studying the storyteller and thought. That lanky fellow has an unsettling resemblance to the leprechaun figure expelled from our house. No! It can't be possible! Brad continued to stand in the doorway and listened to Jake's next tale.

"Well, it goes like this," said Jake. "Pat and Mike wuz sittin' in church. Thir attendance was rather sketchy but that day, Gertie O'Donnel was the soloist and Mike had a likin' for the colleen. Gertie's voice almost reached the hivens and she became so carried away that she lost her balance and fell over the balcony. She had the prisence of mind to grab the chandelier and thir she hung, upside down. The priest, alarmed at the sight of Gertie with her skirts over her head and her pantaloons white as the clouds, for all thir prisent to see, gave a stern warnin'. 'May the first man who turns around be struck blind!'

Mike turns to Pat with his hand over one eye and says, 'Dare I lose an eye?'"

The two men, tears rolling down their cheeks were still laughing and slapping their knees when Brad approached.

Jake, the storyteller, looked up first, blew his nose with a dirty handkerchief and said, "Be you lookin' for someone?"

"Yes," said Brad, "I'm looking for a man who came to my house asking for work."

"I be the one," said Jake.

"Could I have a few words with you, alone?" Brad indicated the picnic table.

"Sure. sure." Jake said to his companion. "Stay right thir, Terry. I've lots more tales to tell, even better than the last."

Brad went straight to the point. "What brought you to my house in Whitby, Jake?"

Jake knit his brows, looked at the table then squinted at Brad. "Like I told yer missus, I wuz lookin' fer work. I saw yer hedge lookin' shabby like and offered to do a trimmin'. I don't charge much."

"You'd better level with me, Jake. Our house is miles from here. You had to take two buses to get there. It doesn't add up."

Jake hitched his dirty trousers. A sly grin preceded his answer. "Yer see," he said, scratching his chin, "I be lookin' for the O'Neils. We became friends on the crossin' from the old sod back in fifty-three or four. We lost touch. Patrick and I were drinkin' buddies. We got thrown out of Molly Nell's bar, by her bouncer, Muldoon. Me and Patrick lay on the dock, dead as two mackerel. I came to first but Patrick was a goner. I panicked and thought, 'The police'll blame me for sure.' So, I jumped onto a ship and hid under a tarp. The captain of the 'Success' found me the next mornin'. I told him I'd owned a dory in Ireland but had come on hard times and moved to Canada with me missus and that she had died in childbirth, so I was at odds. He told me he couldn't pay much. I needed to hide out from the police, so I stayed on."

Patrons at every pub along the way be rememberin' me good cheer. I kept askin' about Patrick's poor widow and it wuz thir I heard the good woman had lost her babe and with her husband gone had come under the care of the good nuns. 'Jake, I says to meself. It be yer Christian duty to try to find that poor colleen and to see to her needs. After all, she wuz a fair lookin' colleen, and bein' we both wuz alone, I got to figurin'. Yer see, it could've been me lyin' dead on the dock." Jake shook his head sadly.

Brad frowned at the implausible story and asked, "When did you say you come to Canada?"

"Well now," Jake scratched his head, wrinkled his brow and finally said, "After World War Two. Like I just said, early fifties. It's been so long…can't rightly say."

Something familiar unnerved Brad. Jake must be between seventy and seventy-five and a powerful man in his younger years. His shirt rode up above strong wrists and his big hands were still strong…laborer's hands.

Jake shifted uneasily at the silence of Brad's scrutiny.

"That's well over fifty years ago, Jake, a long time to try and find someone you barely knew." Brad could almost see the wheels turning in Jake's head as he tried to concoct an answer.

"Mind, it wuzn't steady. I worked me way up the St. Lawrence, finally got bored and hitched the rails to Toronto. Me money ran out and thir wuz hard times. I ended up at the soup kitchen window of 'The Convent of The Good Shepherd.' Those nuns sure treated us right, stews and meat loaves with lots of potatoes and turnips. One day, I met another Irish colleen. We got to talkin', and, 'Yes,' she says, 'there be an

Emma O'Neil but she went some place, Ottawa, Oshawa. That be it, she went to Oshawa.' "That be how I came here. I heard she lived in yer house, so I went thir to look her up. You know, just like a brother, doin' me Christian duty, even after all these years."

"No O'Neil lives in our house. Did you ever marry and get a life of your own?"

"Niver did. Just niver did and that's a fact."

"More to the fact, and more to the point, Jake. You scared my wife by peering in our windows. Never come back! Understand, Jake? If you bother us again, I'll call the police."

"Police! I don't want no truck with police. I wuz just doin' me Christian duty, that's all."

"You'd better be 'doin'' your Christian duty elsewhere, Jake MacNamara."

That said Brad left the open-mouthed Jake sitting at the picnic table.

I sat quietly in our living room and nursed our heavenly-blessed babe when suddenly I felt Grandmother O'Neil's presence. She interrupted my thoughts.

***

"So, Emma Angela be a babe now? Yer a colleen after me own heart."

***

She vanished and I settled my sleeping Emma Angela in our bedroom and went back to the living room. Brad came in and sat on the couch beside me. He poured me a cup of tea and for a few minutes said nothing. He took my hand and barely whispered, "Katie, I had thought we could put all this behind us. Maybe it would be best if we put this house up for sale. It really is quite small for us now with the baby." Suddenly his head jerked upwards.

***

"I heard that, me Boyo," said Grandmother O'Neil. "Niver back away from a fight, especially if it be justified such as this. The divil be dingled, or me name's not, Emma Louise Regan O'Neil. You had the good father bless the yard as well."

***

"We had Father Byrne bless the house," I said. "But since Father Doyle had died, Father Byrne was on his own. He promised to come back and bless our yard when he had time."

***

"Saints preserve me, and Glory be to God for yer house blessin'. Yer safe here! Rest easy. I'll be off with meself, for now."

***

Her vision left. Brad and I looked at each other and in spite of everything shook in laughter. I spilled tea on my wrist and memories of my accident in the cottage in Ireland flooded back. Brad put an aloe leaf on my wrist. It soon healed and we felt much better about our little house. We decided to stay, but we would replace the leprechaun with a statue of St. Francis of Assisi.

Mom slept at our house last night and returned home when Brad came back from Shady Elms. It doesn't seem fair to have her stay here all the time. She protested when I told her my plans but agreed when she saw my unbridled enthusiasm.

I joined a group of mothers in a newly formed exercise class in a house beside the hospital. The arrangement was a good one. Brad dropped Emma and me off on his way to work. The facility for new moms, babes and toddlers was so cheerful that I looked forward to the hours spent there. Emma Angela thrived and bounced with joy as soon as we arrived. They served lunch on a daily basis. Mothers often brought their own favorite treats.

Brad was more relaxed. He often joined us for lunch but today he drove us to Regan's Hardware where my Dad was overjoyed to see us and today greeted us as he often did, "How's my precious angel?"

"I'm fine, Dad," I joked. "And how are you?"

"Katie, you're still a Corker and, Brad, you should bring them here every afternoon and keep up the tradition as I was practically raised beside that cash register. It will work out fine. Gina is here every afternoon and there's even a bed where our big angel can lie down and nurse Emma."

"I don't think that'll work out, Dad. After all, you probably don't have a bed large enough for your *big* angel."

Dad looked disappointed but Brad gave a sigh of relief, and said, "Thanks, Greg, we agree, don't we, Katie? It's a wonderful idea."

Emma Angela was the darling of customers. I parked her in her carriage beside Dad at the cash register. I often busied myself sorting stock with Mom. We were re-arranging glassware and Mom had passed me a set. I stopped mid-reach to the top shelf when I heard a familiar voice on the other side of the aisle. The glasses crashed to the floor.

"I be lookin' fer the O'Neils, Emma in particular. You see, me and her dead husband, Patrick, wuz friends and I heard she moved to this area."

I sucked in my breath and gasped, "That's *him*, the man who came to our door. Emma! Emma! He'll see Emma by the cash register!"

"Everything okay back there, Gina?"

"Yes, Greg," Mom answered, "a minor accident. The stock boy can clean up." She whispered, "I'll create a diversion and get Emma. Sneak behind this row and slip into the storeroom."

I gingerly picked my way over broken glass and made my way as planned. Mom at the cash register smoothly turned the carriage away from the stranger and said. "Come with Nona, Sweetheart." She looked at the man and said, "Good day to you, Sir."

"Thank you, Missus," replied the stranger who called himself Jake MacNamara but looked like Patrick of my nightmares. I shook so badly I was afraid that guy, whoever he is, would hear me. Thank God, Mom didn't say Emma, as he would've gotten the connection immediately. Mom pushed Emma's carriage to the storeroom.

Dad's knit eyebrows showed his alarm. The doorbell tinkled and another customer entered the store. Except it wasn't another customer, it was Brad, here to pick us up.

"WHAT THE HELL ARE YOU DOING HERE, JAKE? Greg, call the police! I warned this guy never to come near us again."

"Hold yer horses, mister! This be a public place, aint it? I not be botherin' you or the missus."

"That's right, Brad." parried Greg. "This gentleman was asking for the O'Neil's."

"I know all about him. I told him at Shady Elms, there are no O'Neils here."

"You don't have to be so testy," said Jake. "I've a right to inquire after me friends, even after all these years." Greg's look of alarm did not go unnoticed by Jake who's face slid into a crafty grin. "Unless, you've somethin' to hide?"

"Listen, you bounder! I've had about enough of your good-for-nothing nonsense. Greg, call the police!"

"Now just a darned minute! I know me rights! Call the police if you dare! You don't have grounds."

"That's right," said Greg. "But this is a place of business and apparently you have none here, so I bid you, good day."

"I be here to do business, all right," warned Jake. He straightened his shoulders and raised himself up to his considerable height. "This aint the end of it. You'll see!"

Greg gave a cautionary look to Brad as Jake turned and strode to the door. They were shaken but Greg was the first to break the silence. "Thank God, there were no customers. Brad, "I don't like it! There's something about him that doesn't ring true. He's here to make trouble and I have a feeling we'll be the recipients."

"Don't worry, Greg. Whoever he is, he's not a match for the Regans and Shaugnnessys." Brad put up his fists in a mock-fight stance that got Greg laughing.

"That's right, Brad. When we put up our dukes, we clear the whole neighborhood. In a serious tone he said, "Our women don't have to know about Jake's threats, agreed."

"Agreed."

Back in the storeroom, Gina heated milk for Katie. "Here, dear. This will calm you. You don't want to upset Emma. Why don't you and Greg come home and have supper with us tonight? Maybe you should even stay over." I nodded in agreement, picked up Emma and held her to my breast to calm my beating heart. She cooed in contentment and my breathing relaxed.

"What was that all about, Greg?" Mom asked.

"Just a drifter who doesn't have any business with us." Greg dismissed the stranger with a wave of his hand. "C'mon gang, my treat, we deserve to eat out tonight. All in favor say yea.

Yea," said Greg. "I vote for all of us."

Dinner wasn't the usual fun-filled-shenanigans. Jake's visit had upset us. Emma fussed and in spite of my parents' pleas, we went home, somewhat relieved as I knew that Jake feared arrest.

16

We settled into a normal routine and one day Siobhan and Tina came for a visit. Tina had moved to Calgary where she worked as a marketing manager. She was the surprise visitor. Siobhan lived nearby and nursed at Lakeridge Health Center where she and Brad frequently crossed paths. Shift work and care for her father left little time for herself.

Time went all too quickly. Words jumbled together as we excitedly tried to catch up. "Remember the time," and, 'It seems like yesterday when we went to high school together," said Siobhan, and, "Yes," said Tina, "and your accident and recovery had us all so worried."

"I try not to think of that." Not all together honestly as I still have a sense of my grandmother.

She seems to return when I need her the most. My eyes clouded over for an instant.

Siobhan noticed and changed the subject. "Remember the time we tried on your grandmother's costumes and you suddenly hovered above us." She realized, too late, that she had touched on a subject that we had vowed to keep secret and both women stared at me. After all these years, they expected an explanation. I was at a loss as to what to say. I knew that as a nurse, Siobhan would have known about out-of-body experiences and since Tina had a full life in Calgary, my story would hold only momentary interest for her.

Except for a few gasps, my friends sat spellbound as I related my visions and nightmares. Tina frowned but Siobhan sat quietly for a few moments and then said, "Your nightmares are rather mystifying though understandable from the trauma you had suffered. What I don't understand is this guy, Jake. Why would he be so interested in finding the O'Neils, mere acquaintances, from long ago?"

Tina asked, "Are there other O'Neils here? Your Dad's family went by Regan."

"That's what's so upsetting. Jake MacNamara looks like the Patrick O'Neil of my nightmares. That and the fact that Jake ended up at Regan's Hardware, puzzles us. He left on what amounted to a threat of police. He has us worried."

"I wish I wasn't so far away," said Tina. "All I can do is pray."

"Thanks, Tina. I wish you were closer too. I miss you guys."

"I'll keep a watch out for him," said Siobhan. "Sooner or later he's bound to end up at hospital in one scrape or another. You never know, Katie, this Jake guy may reveal more than he intends."

Their visit did me more good than I realized. I was content to stay home and look after Emma.

17

Jake MacNamara spent the better part of a week at the library scanning the obituaries with little success. The librarian noted the shabbily dressed man and finally took an interest in him. "Sir, may I be of assistance?"

Jake put on his most affable smile and replied, "Yes, Miss. A fine colleen like yerself must know all about the families hereabouts."

"I have been here for twenty years. Yes, I know of quite a few people. It would be helpful to know what information you are seeking."

"Well," said Jake, screwing up his face in an effort to make the best approach. "You see, Miss, it happened years ago." Jake elaborated in such a sorrowful tone that the librarian, moved by this lonely person trying to do his Christian duty, went out of her way to help him.

"Yes, I do remember hearing of an Emma O'Neil," said the librarian. "It was quite a tragedy, in all the papers. You see, she died from a heart attack four or five years ago, right beside her granddaughter who lay in the snow from an explosion. The dear woman willed her eyes to the eye bank never knowing that her granddaughter would be the recipient. I'll bring up the file. If you want, I'll print off a copy for you. There's a slight charge."

Jake put his head in his hands, rocked back and forth and cried, "Aw, poor, Emma. Poor, Patrick, her long-dead husband, such a long trip to find such sad news."

The librarian, shaken by his outburst, waived the charge and paid for it out of her lunch money. Jake bowed ingratiatingly and slobbered over her hand in an effort to be chivalrous.

He left the library with the information he had sought ever since coming to Oshawa.

Jake whistled all the way from the library back to his digs at Shady Elms with the information under his shirt, and there it would stay until he could put his plan into action. First he had to figure out a plan that would seem likely...until that day when he had a visitor who made his plans do a rapid about-face.

"Hey, Jake!" yelled the avid listener of Jake's jokes. "You've got company."

"That right?" Jake asked, squinting against the sun that put his visitor in shadow. The figure looked somewhat familiar and Jake moved farther into the 'Common Room' to have a better look. His hand clutched the side of the card table as realization struck him full force. There, stood, Jake MacNamara! It can't be! He must have a twin!

The real Jake MacNamara approached and the imposter stared open-mouthed and nearly fell over when Jake said. "How've you been, Patrick, ould sot?"

Jake, the imposter looked around, to see if they were being observed, and nervously chewed his lip. "I think we be needin' a little drink 'efore we talk." He indicated his room down the hall.

The two men sat across from each other, one on the bed and the new Jake, who had pulled up a chair, straddled it and waited to hear the blarney he knew was to come.

"Almost seems like old times," joked Patrick, nervously thinking about the information under his shirt and how this turn of events could be worked to his advantage.

"Cut the crap, Patrick," said Jake MacNamara. "You left me fer dead, took all me money and stole me identity. I ended up in jail for abandonment of that son you sired with that Bridget Connolley you met at Molly's bar. She knew you had split so she came after me for child support. I didn't have a leg to stand on as I had yer identity and there weren't no picture or fingerprints to prove otherwise, Patrick O'Neil."

"Now, Jake, simmer down. I thought you wuz stone, cold dead. I knew I'd be blamed. Yer money wouldn't be any good to you if you wuz dead, now then, would it, Jake?"

"Shove your blarney up your arse, Patrick O'Neil. You owe me big time, you good for nothin' bounder, and I intend to collect, one way or t'other."

"Simmer down, Jake," parried Patrick. "Just hold yer horses. I've got a plan."

"Yeah, I bet yer've a plan all right and so have I. Me plan is to get you locked up for stealin' me identity and for all the money it cost me raisin' yer son, that's what, YER SON."

"Hold on a minute, Jake, while I shows how we'll both be winners," said Patrick, patting his newfound evidence. He pulled out the copies of newspaper clippings.

"What's that got to do with us?"

"I'll show you what that has to do with us. Me Emma remarried and we niver wuz divorced."

"So," said Jake MacNamara, unconvinced, "She thought you wuz dead."

"Yeah? Well I wuzn't and I be here to collect, *big time*. She robbed me of me son and then married that rich guy, Sean Regan. He had a big business that he left to his son, Greg. That business be rightfully mine. At least half be rightfully mine and I intend to fight fer it."

"You'll have a pretty hard time when you've blathered me name all over town. ME name!"

"We can work that out, Jake," pleaded Patrick. "Every one always said we wuz like two peas in a pod. We can pull it off! I know we can! Trust me, Jake, and you'll see."

"*Trust!* You don't know the meanin'! You always were pretty good with the blarney, Patrick O'Neil. Now let this be yer warnin'. Pull a fast one on me, and you'll end up in Lake Ontario."

"Niver mind the nigative, Jake," said Patrick. "I've the powers and this little scrap o' green," Patrick pulled Katie's bikini from his pocket, "will be mighty handy for me powers."

"What the hell are you doin' with a colleen's bloomers? You're either tetched or obsessed."

"Me lucky charm, Jake, me foin friend, been in me pocket four years. Found it in the Regan's bushes, along with this ividence." He patted his chest. "We be on the winnin' track."

"You silly old fool! Yer tetched. You've been carryin' that dirty rag for four years? Show me the luck, Patrick. Yer blarney be better'n yer brains."

"Niver mind wastin time natterin,' Jake. Let's drink to our success. For now, we'd better keep up the charade until we get new digs. Then you can be you and I be me."

The two clinked glasses in renewed friendship and settled into plans for a lucrative future. They walked out in the sunlight slapping each other's backs and telling jokes just like the old days and found new lodgings around the corner on Olive Avenue.

The widow, an absentee landlady, sized them up and bought their long-lost brother story. "Yes" they'd be willing to share the sitting room with attached bath. "No" they didn't need to cook as they had made other arrangements. A buck paid for a meal at St. Vincent's Kitchen.

She accepted one month's rent and said she'd be by to check. If satisfactory, she'd collect the next month's rent. She warned. "I'll not be toleratin' drink or carousin' in my house."

Satisfied, they moved into their new digs where Patrick introduced his plan. "First," said the ever-so-sly, Patrick, "we be needin' to work on yer appearance."

"Niver mind me appearance," said Jake in a huff. "Take a look at yerself. You look like you dug yer clothes out o' a garbage bin."

"Now, now, Jake, don't be gettin' testy. We'll come to the clothes part later. I think yuz need to shave off yer lip hair."

"Niver! Yer the one that should have a moustache."

"Can't yer see, Jake? If I grow a moustache, I'll be noticed."

"Are yer daft, Patrick?" You wuz already noticed as me. Now yer have to be noticed fer yourself. So yer the one that has to grow the moustache."

"Then we both be havin' moustaches?" Patrick scratched his head. "Doesn't make sense."

They argued back and forth until Patrick finally convinced Jake to do it his way for the sake of the fortune they would come into when he claimed his proper share of Emma's estate. Jake shaved his moustache and took a critical look at the white skin under his nose.

"And now, you blitherin' smartarse, what do yer think I'll do about this white streak?"

"Quit yer yappin', Jake, 'til yer gits the whole picture," said Patrick, standing beside Jake looking at their images in the mirror. "Do you see it now, Jake? We looks enough alike to be brothers...after a few minor adjustments."

"Yeah, what adjustments?" Jake asked suspiciously.

"Well, like yuz need to put lifts in yer shoes to bring yer height up to mine."

"Thir's nothin' the matter with me height, Patrick, me lad. I can beat yer clock any day."

"Now who's the daft one, eh, Jake? I'm not talkin' 'bout fightin'. I'm talkin' 'bout matchin' yer looks to mine. Yer got to be seen around the places where I've been, like walkin' in front o' Regan's Hardware and havin' a look in the windows."

"Tell me, Patrick. What in hell good'll that do?"

"It'll establish yer identity as yerself, that's what it'll do. Jake. Yer'll have to go to the places where I wuz seen. For instance, I'll give yer directions to that nice librarian. You've got to go back and thank her for all her help. For this ividence, and our fortune, settin' on this here table. Now, Jake, take another look in the mirror and for gawd's sake stop maulin' that white streak above yer lip. Here, try on me cap. There now, Jake, yer gettin' to look more and more like yerself every minute. We just have to lay low for a spell and work on me plan."

"Yer plan, Patrick, sure as hell better be a good un. You owe me big time and I intend to collect. I be the one that supported that son of yers over the years and I now hear that he has a son o' his own. I niver did tell him you wuz his da. I keep that little ace-in-the-hole. Be warned, Patrick, me boyo. You did it to me once. You'll niver do it agin!"

"Settle down, Jake! Fer gawd's sake, settle down. We'll finish first on this one."

"We'd better, Patrick, we'd better!"

"And, that we will. Now cool yer jets, Jake, and we'll have a nip to celebrate."

They drank until they were as drunk as two skunks and did not see the light of day until the next morning where they finalized their plans.

Patrick said, "I don't rightly have the right duds fer our plan. Give me yer cash."

Jake reluctantly forked over the bucks they needed to buy matching suits at Goodwill, and under Patrick O'Neil's tutelage, Jake visited the librarian and startled her with a profusion of blubbered thanks ending with a slobbery kiss to her hand, as per Patrick's instructions.

'Remember Jake, yer have to be like me, as yer former charmin' self.'

Over confident that his charade had worked, Jake decided to take a little stroll to Regan's Hardware. He peered in the windows and found the displays 'mighty interestin'. Patrick had neglected to warn him not to go into the store so Jake's curiosity took him inside.

When the door bell jingled, Greg looked up from his post behind the cash register and gasped as the familiar figure of Jake walking right past him to the back of the store. There he stood looking up at the display of antique saws.

Greg, grabbed the startled Jake by the arm, spun him around and yelled, "You! get the hell out of my store! This time, I *will* call the police. You were warned last time. *Get out!*'

Jake stared at Greg in disbelief. He quickly tried to recover. "Sir, you must have me confused with someone else. I've niver been here 'efore."

"Don't try to fool me, Jake MacNamara," said Greg. "I'd know your face and that Irish accent of yours anywhere. You've been warned more than once. I'll not have you scaring my daughter and intimidating us any more. If I see your face again, you'll be charged with public mischief. NOW, GET, before I call the police!"

Jake MacNamara made a hasty retreat and vowed as he ran back to their digs. I'm gonna give that damned Patrick the tarrin' of his life. That bounder niver said a thing about not goin' in. He must be up to somethin'. He kicked the door open, stormed up to Patrick and punched him in the nose.

"Why the hell did you do that?" Patrick demanded grabbing a towel over his spurting nose.

"That's fer settin' me up, Patrick, me lad. You niver told me you wuz warned to stay away from Regan's Hardware. I damned near got arrested. That's what that's fer. That and this!"

Jake yanked Patrick by his arm, spun him around and gave him another haymaker. The punch knocked Patrick back on the couch. He quickly rolled over, leaned down and jerked Jake's legs out from under him. They wrestled around knocking over chairs, swearing and threatening each other until they heard pounding on their door.

"NO FIGHTIN' IN THIS BUILDIN'!" shouted the voice in the hall. "Didn't you hear what the landlady said? You'll get thrown out on your asses."

"Now, see what yer did," hissed Patrick his voice muffled by the towel.

"See what *I did*, Patrick, you bounder! You darned near got me thrown in jail, that's what *you did.*"

"You didn't go into Regan's Hardware, Jake? I told you to just walk by, casual like…like yer takin' a stroll and maybe look in the windows. I wuz warned, not to go into Regan's Hardware. But that Greg Regan and his fiery son-in-law don't be ownin' the sidewalk."

"NOW YOU TELL ME! You better level with me, Patrick, or heed me warnin'. or it's more than a bloody nose fer you, more like a swim in Davey's locker."

Patrick's head pounded and his bloody nose throbbed. He sat disgruntled and eyed the suspicious Jake. Then he smiled at what the imagined the outcome of Jakes's little visit inside Regan's could have been. I can see it all now, Jake, all decked out in prison orange, a color surely to rankle his Dublin upbringin'.

"Wipe that stupid grin of yer face, Patrick O'Neil. You must be up to somthin'."

"No, Jake. Everythin's turnin' out just the way I planned. Now that Greg Regan will niver put two and two togither when I show up and present him with the facts. The very facts that'll make us rich and him poor."

"Yer a sly one, Patrick. Let's drink on that, shall we?"

"Don't mind if we do, Jake, don't mind if we do. You see, we'll be rich as potato farmers in Prince Edward Island."

They toasted to their success then Patrick said. "I be thinkin', we need a bit of legal advice, just to be on the safe side but I'll need to handle that part meself, if you don't mind, Jake?"

"Much obliged," said Jake affably as the prospect of being rich mingled with whiskey evoked a most pleasing be-muddled taste of success. "Patrick, me lad, you warms me Christian soul."

Patrick stood before the law offices of H. G. Dunbar, Barrister and Solicitor. He straightened his shoulders, unaccustomed to the newly acquired business suit from Goodwill, and strode to the door with confidence.

"Do you have an appointment with Mr. Dunbar?" inquired Rose, his secretary.

"No. Miss,...but I be here of urgent impertenance. I be lookin' fer, me iver lovin', wife,

Emma Louise O'Neil." Patrick picked up and pocketed the lawyer's card for future reference.

Rose opened her mouth in shock then covered it as her smile threatened to erupt at the man's misuse of the word. She nervously looked to Mr. Dunbar's open door as he approached the stranger with a practiced blank expression that belied his curiosity, and asked, "Sir, how may I help you?"

"Ahem!" Patrick cleared his throat and glanced at the secretary, "You see, it be a private and sensitive nature."

"I see, Mister, what did you say your name was, Sir?"

"Patrick O'Neil." I be Patrick O'Neil, iver lovin', husband of Emma Louise O'Neil."

"Please, come into my office, Mr. O'Neil." Mr. Dunbar directed him to a chair. "Please, be frank, Mr. O'Neil. What is the purpose of your visit?"

"Well you see," said Patrick earnestly, "Emma Louise O'Neil was me, iver lovin', missus. She thought I be dead and some years later, I hears she be marryin' a Sean Regan. Of course, me bein' still alive and all, she could be been charged with bigamine."

"I believe you mean bigamy, Mr. O'Neil. Please continue." Mr. Dunbar urged, already suspicious of this crafty character.

"It be like this," said Patrick. "She owes me. Her leavin' and getting rich and all, and me, her iver lovin', husband just strugglin' to get by."

"So, Mr. O'Neil...It *is* about money."

"Well...not entirely."

Patrick went on to tell the story of the worst hurt of all, she had robbed him of a son, a son that he later found out was raised by someone else.

Mr. Dunbar put a stop to Patrick O'Neil's tale of woe. "I knew your former wife, very well. I was her lawyer on all matters. You were legally, declared dead, and so legally, Emma Louise O'Neil had the right to remarry after the required time. She was not a bigamist, Mr. O'Neil, but a very up-standing citizen, well respected by all who knew her. You had many years to make it known to her that you were still alive but obviously..."

"Now, just a damned minute, mister, know-it-all lawyer," interrupted Patrick. "I know me rights!"

"I repeat, Mr. O'Neil. You obviously had years to look up, 'yer iver lovin', wife, as you put it, but chose not to. I suggest you take your bag of tricks back to wherever you came from."

"Bag of tricks, is it? You'll see!" Patrick scrambled out of the chair.

Mr. Dunbar stood up. "Your shenanigans haven't gone undetected. You've been warned to stay away from the Shaughnessys and Regan's Hardware. Your snooping around in the past for your own personal gain has been reported and if you continue to bother this family ever again, I personally will defend their rights to be free of your continued harassment. Good day."

Patrick stormed out of Dunbar's law office and went straight to a pub where he drank himself into a stupor. He failed to show up at the digs to give a report to Jake so Jake came looking for and found him.

"Patrick!" Jake shook his arm. "What in hell're you doin' here? Yer supposed to give me the good news, not go celebratin' on yer own."

"News? Whash news?" Patrick's bloodshot eyes looked at the two Jakes swaying before him. He shook his head in disbelief, for up above Jake he saw his Emma. She looked rather misty but he had to ask, "Is that you, Emma, me iver lovin',wife?"

"Don't be daft," Jake said. "You're drunk as a skunk. Of course, I'm not Emma. I be Jake!"

***

"That's right, Patrick, yer iver lovin', wife. He be Jake all right, and I be Emma, here to tell you what a fool you be and to give you fair warnin', Patrick O'Neil. Niver mess with me family again or by all the saints in hiven, you'll have much to answer for."

***

"Aw, Emma, me long-lost luv. I be yearnin' for yuz after all these years and here yer be, before me very eyes, a hiven-sent-blessin'." Patrick reached toward Emma but grasped Jake's lapels.

"The only thing before yer eyes is goin' to be me fist," Jake warned and yanked Patrick off the bar stool and across Simcoe to their digs on Olive. Jake shoved Patrick onto a chair and threw a pitcher of cold water over his head.

126

"Now, look what yuz done!" yelled Patrick. "All over me nice suit."

"You mean all over *me* nice suit." Jake yelled. "Sober up and tell me what happened 'efore I punch out yer lights."

"Jush a darned minute! Firsh, give me 'nother drink," Patrick pleaded.

"Here!" Jake said as he poured another pitcher of water over Patrick's head. "Be that enough drink or would you like some more?"

"Firsh, I be needin' a wee rest," lisped Patrick, stalling for time, slumping over the table.

"You'll get a rest all right, Patrick O'Neil, *eternal rest,* if you don't level with me, after all the time and money I've invested on yer account and how we wuz both gonna get rich."

Patrick struggled to gain sobriety and finally slumped into unconsciousness. Jake left him in disgust, put on a suit and looked in the mirror. 'Just like two peas in a pod.' He patted the papers in his suit pocket, determined to take matters in his own hands. He walked briskly up the street to Regan's Hardware. He wasn't afraid of that Greg Regan. He had the evidence in his pocket that would make him rich. He looked enough like Patrick O'Neil to be Patrick O'Neil. In fact, *I am Patrick O'Neil.*

Confidence bolstered he pushed open the door and said to a startled Greg Regan. "I be Patrick O'Neil, and I be here to collect me inheritance."

"Your inheritance! What in hell are you talking about? Get out of my store. I warned you before, Jake MacNamara."

"It might not be your store fer long."

"Cut the crap, Jake! The jig's up! Mr. Dunbar said you were up to no good."

Jake knit his brows for a moment at this turn of events. Damn, I niver did get the goods out of that drunken bounder, Patrick."

Greg pushed the button under the counter that signaled the police station and within minutes a chilling and familiar sound of a siren sent shivers up Jake's spine. He turned to go out the door and was met by two police officers. They escorted him to the sidewalk with a warning to never go to Regan's store again.

Jake shouldered his way through the curious crowd and ran down Simcoe Street to their digs to have it out with Patrick. Patrick wasn't there! Jake slammed the door and strode across Simcoe to the bar where he grabbed the startled Patrick by the scruff of the neck, shoved him out the door and began to pound the crap out of him. They scuffled and swore and finally reached the Canadian Pacific Railway overpass. Jake landed a haymaker on the drunken Patrick who lost his footing and rolled down the embankment beside the tracks.

"Glory, be to God! I've killed the drunken sot!" Exclaimed Jake looking around, to see if they had been noticed. Seeing no one, Jake leaned over and removed Patrick's I.D and the lawyer's card from his suit pocket and replaced them with his own I.D. "Tit for tat, Patrick, me lad. When you reach the pearly gates, I hope you remembers you stole me identity. Now I be havin' yers and I intend to make it good fer me. Just like we planned, Paddy, ould chum." Jake gave Patrick a few pats on the cheek and scrambled up the embankment.

Finding the coast clear, Jake took the back streets to their digs. He threw his few belongings in a knapsack, put on Patrick's Blue Jays cap, and with solitary purpose boarded a bus and got a transfer to Whitby. You'll niver best me again, Patrick, ould chum. The Lord have mercy on yer cheat'n' soul, efore yer arrives at the undertakers in a used suit, with nowhere to go.

18

"Give me a drag," said Buddy the eight-year-old under the bridge.

"You're too young to smoke," declared the older lad with annoying superiority.

"Yeah, Gus?" Well, we'll just see about that when I tell Dad." He leaned over and took the butt. It was then that he saw a foot sticking up out of the long grass. He dropped the butt.

Gus yelled and slapped the grass with his baseball cap. "Hey, Buddy! Are you trying to set the whole place on fire? I told you that you wuz too young to smoke."

"Gus! Look! A foot's stickin' outta the grass, over there, by the tracks. I think it's a body!" They got up to investigate and Buddy said, "He looks pretty dead to me. We'd better split!"

"Stay cool, Buddy, and don't be such a sissy, he's dressed in a suit and tie. Maybe there's a reward. First, let's find out who he is."

Gus knelt on the grass and began to poke into Patrick O'Neil's pockets. Patrick stirred and said "Jake! Jake!"

The boys jumped back and Gus said, "He's Jake! He just called his name!" They dug out the I. D. cards. Gus announced, "He's Jake, all right, Jake MacNamara. He lives round the corner. Jake moaned. "Don't worry, Jake, said Gus, "we'll call 911 and soon you'll be okay. I'll stay here with him, Buddy, while you scramble up the embankment and call 911. There's a pay phone down the street."

"But, Gus, I don't have a quarter."

"Well, he does!" said Gus, jerking his thumb towards Patrick. He knelt and dug in Patrick's pocket, found a quarter and gave it to his kid brother.

Siobhan was working in emergency when the ambulance brought Patrick to the hospital. The patient was in bad shape. The bruise on his jaw looked like it might be broken. He reeked of liquor and had a rip in the knee of what had been a presentable-looking suit. However, there was no I.D. The patient kept saying, "Jake! Jake!"

A sudden awareness came over Siobhan that he might be the same Jake, the one who had been harassing Katie and her family. She had seen Brad in the cafeteria, and surmised that he was still on duty. She paged him to see if he had a few minutes, that it was important that he come to emergency. Perhaps he could identify the stranger.

Brad took one look at Patrick's drunken form and said, "That's him, Jake MacNamara, the guy who's been stalking our house and Regan's Hardware. Where was he found?"

"Two brothers had been walking along the railroad tracks when they thought they discovered a body. When they found out he was alive, they phoned 911."

"Where's his I.D.?" Brad asked.

"He didn't have any on him, at least according to the boys."

"He probably had I.D., all right. The kids took it, probably hoping they'd collect a reward. I'll pay them a visit and make their dreams come true."

Brad's visit to the home of the boys was well worth the forty bucks it cost. Jake MacNamara's I.D. confirmed his suspicions.

He later reported to Katie, "Jake won't bother us any more. He's in for a long recovery with a broken leg."

The real Jake swaggered with confidence as he strode up Dunbar's walk. He held Patrick O'Neil's I.D. and vowed revenge on him.

I'll scam him out of the inheritance he hoped to claim and take it for meself. I deserve it for all the trouble that damn blarney-spoutin' cussed sot caused me. Cursed be the day I iver met his sorry soul on that damned ship, 'The Free Spirit.' Rather has a nice ring to it. That's me, from now on, a free spirit. He approached Mr. Dunbar's secretary and said. "Me and yer buddy, lawyer in thire's got business, Miss."

Mr. Dunbar emerged from his office and said, "And what business may that be, Sir?"

"Me name's Patrick O'Neil," said Jake with bolstered confidence, and struck out this hand for the welcome he expected.

Mr. Dunbar's hand remained at his side. He gave a quick glance to Rose and with a slight cautionary shake of his head motioned to this fellow who also claimed to be Patrick O'Neil to come into his office, thinking, This might be an amusing anecdote to end an uninteresting day.

Jake sat in the chair indicated by Mr. Dunbar, noted the slight smile of encouragement and asked, "Mind if I smoke?"

"As a matter of fact, I do," said Mr. Dunbar.

Jake stuck his fixings back in his pocket and launched into his sorry tale. Mr. Dunbar heard him out until Jake was almost bereft of explaining about his long-sought-for, 'iver lovin', wife,' Emma Louise O'Neil. Mr. Dunbar cleared his throat and held up his hand for this new Patrick to desist. He said. "Mr. O'Neil, or whoever you claim to be, I warn you to go no further with this charade. You are the second Patrick O'Neil claiming to be the long-lost husband of Emma Louise O'Neil. There will be no fortune for you or for your accomplice who came here the other day with the same scam. I also warn you, as I did him, that he can and will be charged as will you."

Jake screwed up his face in disbelief. That damned Patrick has done it to me ag'in. He knew right well what this smart-Alec lawyer said and he didn't give me a hint.

"Do I make myself perfectly clear?" Mr. Dunbar said rising to end the charade.

"Well, thir must be some mistake," Jake said trying to cover lost ground. "That other guy, who called himself Patrick O'Neil, is an imposter."

"It looks that you both have made more than one mistake. As I said before," Mr. Dunbar raised his voice, "Be warned! Don't ever come back here or near my clients again or I shall personally see that you end up in jail along with the many embezzlers before you. Good day."

"Damn that Patrick's cursed soul! May he burn feriver," Jake cussed as he stormed past the secretary, out the door and onto the street. "To hell with Patrick and to hell with this cursed town. Now I have his cussed identity and mine be on his dead body. I need a drink."

Jake sat in the nearest pub, ordered beer, fish and chips and absently looked at the six o'clock news.

Bulletin: Man left for dead by the railroad tracks on Simcoe South. He was found by two youths. In spite of his drunken condition and the fact that he had a broken leg, it looks like he will recover. Police are looking for the assailant of Jake MacNamara. Mr. MacNamara is about sixty-five to seventy-five years, graying hair and speaks with a heavy Irish accent. If you have any information about this man, please call 911.

"Well I be a Corker, if thir iver wuz one!" Jake said as he slammed his beer on the table. His out-burst drew attention he no longer sought so he threw a few bucks on the table and mumbled to himself. When I gets ahold of him, I'll break his t'other leg. I think me needs a visit to the hospital to claim me long-lost brother.

Shaughnessys and Regans also watched the news bulletin with interest and relief. That Jake MacNamara fellow would not be bothering them again. Brad had identified him at the hospital.

The I.D. that he had purchased from the boys confirmed that, indeed, that person found by the railroad tracks was, Jake MacNamara.

Katie gave a sigh of relief and was the first to speak. "It's sad that a person would turn out that way but I'm so relieved he won't bother us again."

"Mr. Dunbar will see to that," said Brad. "He's assured both your Dad and me that he'll press charges on our behalf...and that we would win."

"That's right," said Greg as he reached for Gina's hand. Let's throw a party to celebrate the end of that nuisance."

19

Siobhan was working in emergency when Irene, said, "Siobhan, take a look at that guy by the information window. I thought he was admitted with a broken leg. You know, the guy those kids found down by the tracks."

Siobhan studied the tall man from her position in emergency. He leaned over, talking to the nurse through the sliding window. She opened her mouth in disbelief. I can almost swear that he is the person we admitted a few days ago. I'll wait until he leaves and inquire from Velma what he wanted.

"Do you mean," Velma asked, "that old man going through those doors? He said the guy who was found by the tracks is his long-lost brother. His name is Patrick O'Neil. I sent him to room three twenty seven."

Siobhan sucked in her breath and telephoned Brad who was working in the lab. "Brad, I hope you're sitting down! A man who claims to be Patrick O'Neil and long-lost brother to Jake MacNamara has gone up to pay him a visit. At first, I thought he was the same Jake MacNamara. They look so much alike."

Brad made his way to the room, slipped behind a curtain and watched the unbelievable scenario. The patient sitting up in bed looked up, mouth open, ready for his spoon-filled yogurt when his visitor swatted the yogurt out of his hand. The spoon clattered on the floor and yogurt splattered on the surprised face of the patient who said, "Jake MacNamara! What in hell did you do that fer! You left me fer dead and stole me I. D. cards."

"Just like you did to me those many years ago, "Patrick O'Neil. Yer little charade's up, ould chum. Thir's no fortune for either of us. You didn't tell me you wuz at that smart-Alec lawyer's office, did you, Patrick, me boy?"

"Well, I wuz gonna, Jake. You know that! You just didn't give me a chance, that's all."

"Thire'll be no more chances for the likes o' you, Patrick O'Neil. I ought to break yer other leg for the trouble you caused me from the day we met. A curse on yer damned cheatin' soul."

"Now, Jake, just give me 'nother chance. When I get out of here..."

"Jake cut him off. "You used up all yer chances, Patrick O'Neil. I want me identity! Give it to me, *or else!*"

"Hold yer horses, Jake. It be right here in the drawer."

Jake opened the drawer and Patrick pulled the cord for the nurse. All hell broke loose. Jake grabbed his own I.D. and shoved Patrick out of bed onto the floor. He turned to escape Patrick's shrieks and ran into Brad and two burly male nurses.

Police arrived, cuffed Jake and took him to the station where he was charged with false identity, bodily harm to a patient and causing a disturbance.

Patrick O'Neil was the worse for wear and was served with similar charges, except for causing bodily harm, and ended up with both legs in traction. He chuckled to himself at the thought. Jake MacNamara, wearin' the orange, rottin' in jail and not the green of his choosin'.

"Emma, Emma, me love." Patrick pleaded to his only visitor, the vision of his, 'iver lovin', wife, who's smug smile nearly drove him crazy. "It's all yer fault, Emma. It's all yer fault. Get away from me and let me suffer in peace."

***

"The only peace you'll iver have, Patrick, me, 'iver lovin, husband,' is when you make amends for all the harm you caused to me granddaughter, Katie, and her family. I tell you, Patrick, that you'll niver have rest 'til you make amends."

***

"Nurse! Nurse!" Patrick shouted frantically and rang for the nurse. "Get her away from me! I tell you, she's here to haunt me! Get her away!" Patrick picked up his glass of water and threw it at Emma's presence hovering over his bed.

The glass crashed to the floor and two male nurses hurried into the room. "What did I tell you, Zack? This guy has lost it! That's the third time he's thrown his water glass across the room. He imagines he sees his dead wife."

"Is you daft?" Patrick screamed. "I see her! She's right thir! Yer both blind!" He grabbed his eyeglasses. They sailed past the face of the burly attendant, who was trying to calm him down, and smashed on the floor.

"Easy there, mister! Calm down!"

Patrick saw the needle coming toward his arm. He flailed about as best he could until he was finally subdued and slumped down into the bed, mouth agape.

"Know this guy, Brad?" Zack asked.

"No! I don't know him but he's been around town stirring up trouble for the last few years."

Peace has finally settled over our house. We hope we've seen the last of Jake MacNamara who is serving his sentence in minimum security in Lindsay. When the judge asked him if he had anything to say in his defense, Jake had declared, "I need me head read listenin' to that damned, Patrick O'Neil and all his schemes, as empty as a balloon full o' blarney."

We hear that Jake has adjusted to prison life, in spite of his 'wearin' o' the orange.' He's such a constant source of amusement to the other prisoners with his many jokes and shenanigans that the whole atmosphere has changed to one of camaraderie. Jake is giving lessons on the Jews' Harp and on the fine art of step dancing. Even the guards are practicing for their Christmas and Hanukah Concert.

As for Patrick O'Neil, I have reason to believe Grandmother Emma

Regan O'Neil will keep him occupied for the rest of his days. His insistence that she haunts him, followed by his throwing tantrums got him permanent lodgings in 'Extenda-Care.'

The statue of St. Frances of Assisi stands by our little pond. It is a pleasure to take Emma Angela for a walk in our garden. She waves her little hands and kicks her feet when she sees the saint's statue just as she did when she had seen the leprechaun. Yes, we had our yard blessed. My grandmother's comforting presence has dispelled my bad dreams. I have a feeling that she'll come again if I really need her. That is, if she isn't too busy with 'her iver lovin'.

The End